Also by D.S. Milne
Road Kill
'Ino 'ino

YELLOW FOX

By

D.S. Milne

Caveat Lector

The characters and events portrayed in Yellow Fox are fictitious.

The setting: Somewhere in New Mexico.

The author has taken certain liberties embellishing the landscape.

Any similarities to real persons, living or dead, is purely

coincidental and not intended by the author.

There are disguised descriptions throughout the text naming a specific area, however, the reader should

realize they are merely a figment of the author's imagination to set the scene thusly.

Order this book online at www.trafford.comor email orders@trafford.com

Most Trafford titles are also available at major online book retailers.

Printed in Victoria, BC, Canada.

ISBN: 978-1-4269-2015-8 (sc)

ISBN: 978-1-4269-2016-5 (hc)

Library of Congress Control Number: 2009913211

Our mission is to efficiently provide the world's finest, most comprehensive book publishing service, enabling every author to experience success. To find out how to publish your book, your way, and have it available worldwide, visit us online at www.trafford.com

Trafford rev. 6/3/2010

 www.trafford.com

North America & international
toll-free: 1 888 232 4444 (USA & Canada)
phone: 250 383 6864 ♦ fax: 812 355 4082

In Memory

Clarise

YELLOW FOX

In the Hopi tradition Yellow Fox is called *Sikyaatayo*.
The Navajo use the words **T**itso maiittsooi.

The Hopis make a habit to hunt the yellow fox. They stalk the animal for it's pelts. After stretching the hide out on the ground, they let it dry. The Kachinas then wear the pelt dangling from the rear waist. Some Kachinas also employ it as a ruff. According to Hopi mythology Taawa, the Sun God, places the yellow fox skin on a ladder pole at his home. At that time it gets to be Yellow Dawn.

According to an ancient Indian legend, Yellow Fox was a symbol of heroism. Another tale relates that *Pitsinsivostiyo* (Cotton Seed Boy) an unattractive young man, loses his wife to *Sikyaatayo* as the two join in an adulterous episode. It seems his wife had set a condition that she would not marry any of her many suitors until one brought her a live yellow fox. Cotton Seed Boy, with the aid of his grandmother, managed to capture a yellow fox and thereby won the hand of his beautiful bride.

However, she had eyes for the handsome Sikyaatayo, from another tribe, and gave herself readily to his advances.

Cotton Seed boy was devastated and implored his people to destroy Sikyaatayo's village, killing the men and boys and taking captive the women and girls. Yellow Fox was slain by an arrow in the melee.

CHAPTER ONE

Jack scratched an old itch. He was traveling along a nameless one lane asphalt road, crossing a huge wasteland, barren and without a hint of any other humanity.

The dog had been on the trail for days, it seemed. His throat was parched and his feet were sore beyond imagination. There was a small pond. He lapped the stale water but briefly and then shook his head furiously—jowls smacking against teeth. It would be many more miles before he tasted sweet water.

The day was contemplating night as the sun disappeared behind a large mesa having completed it's assigned duty for the day. Ahead was a black strip of a road. It would be easier walking for the animal. He sat in the middle of the asphalt too weary to go much further. A vehicle approached. Maybe he could adopt the humans within and they would feed and water his wracked body.

The truck's headlights swept over the dog —very black—squatting in the road, unconcerned, unafraid, aloof. The pickup was in *his* territory. Jack swerved to avoid the animal and yelled at it through his window. His words were being used up on deaf ears.

A bit further along, the shadow of a man walking in his direction took up most of the road's shoulder. As Jack slowed, he saw that the figure was draped in a tattered serape-looking piece of material; a knapsack was slung over one shoulder.

He stopped, and then backed up. Some company would be welcome.

He rolled down the passenger-side window.

"Where ya headed?"

"Don't rightly know."

"Okay. Climb in, we'll go somewhere."

He had the appearance of a man returning to his hometown to attend his own funeral.

He wasn't a tall man. He wasn't a thin man. He used every effort to not appear short nor squat—and almost convinced Jack.

"Name's Jack."

"That's good."

"What's yours?"

"Why? You some nosy critter or something?" he answered with an enigmatic smile.

"Nope. Just like to know what kinda baggage I'm haulin'".

"Well, I ain't no hetaera, if that's what you're thinking! Anyhow, let's back up and pick up the cur. He looks like he needs a ride too."

"You sure don't mind ordering people around after just meeting them, Chief."

"Ain't no Chief!" He looked askance at Jack, studying him. "How's about hydrating me."

"What?"

"Got any water?"

"In the canteen. Help yourself. How far to the next town?" Jack asked, not expecting a reasonable answer.

"Must be more than fifty-miles, I'd guess—and I still ain't no Chief."

"Alright, already. Didn't mean to start an Indian uprising. Get your door open and we'll corral that dog."

The ancient one helped the foot-sore animal into the cab, talking some kind of gibberish to it. It was a three or four-year old Labrador.

"We'll call him Midnight. That's about what time it be and besides, he's black as anthracite."

"I don't care. Just so you keep him on your side. I don't need that stinking mutt turning into a lap dog and trying to help me drive."

"This here's a full-blooded animal. Musta run off from somewheres."

"You some kinda dog expert?" Jack managed.

"Not really, just a good guesser. Half the time I might be right. The trouble is, I don't know which half."

They traveled a quiet twenty miles, or so.

"What's that up ahead, Chief? I see some lights." He grinned inwardly. This should get a rise out of his passenger for calling him Chief.

Not even the hint of a sneer.

"It could be maybe some kinda town," he answered, with a grimace. "Still ain't no damned Chief," he mumbled half to himself.

"I thought you told me we were more than fifty miles from the closest place."

"I know nothing of this place," he replied, patting the broad head of the dog.

A few miles further on they were in sight of a small community. The sign at the edge of town was a masterpiece of distraction:

Welcome to **Estancia al Cabo**
The most beautiful spot in New Mexico

The first tentative rays of sunlight cleared the eastern horizon. The sky changed from purple to a clear, light blue. Quite beautiful to the casual observer. It was an extraordinary entrance for the new day.

They espied a ramshackle café made out of shitty-looking plaster. Adjacent to it, inconspicuous, colorless huts and lean-to's slink for a short stretch—dun, gray, taupe, flimsy, unassumingly low—as if ashamed or afraid to impose on the remainder of the community.

The town was all that remained of a once prosperous Estancia where a wealthy Spanish family had once lived off the land and the toil of Indian slaves.

The next reasonable excuse for a permanent building was the combination mercantile and cantina. It was erected of coursed adobe slabs made of gooey mud laid on top of one another and sported a thatched roof porch. A lamb, flayed except for it's head, hung upside down from a rough beam.

Chili ristras and several ears of maize hung from lintels of the makeshift porch. Seed jars, lined up like soldiers, rested on a plank table. The weathered wooden sign over the entrances had a lacuna between the two words *Tienda* and *Cantina* as though a woodpecker had had a snack while perched thereon. The vaguely readable letters were roughly carved in the aging wood.

There was a historical whiff about the place.

Located further down the street was a livery barn that housed a combination blacksmith shop and garage; a twelve-unit motel; a small weathered church, it's steeple naked of a bell. It had been carried off by the Spaniards to make cannons, many years ago.

The Estancia and adjacent town were in absolute disrepair, the whole of which nestled on a shelf of land beside a large, dry arroyo. The place hadn't been built—rather it happened.

"Whaddya say we pull in and grab some breakfast?" Jack asked.

"I'd enjoy that, very much, but it seems I don't have the wherewithal for a meal."

"That's okay. I need some company. Might even treat the mutt."

"That would be most generous, Jack."

The three new-found chums entered the café and took up residence at a table near the front door. Juanita, the owner, brought them two mugs of coffee and a pan of water for Midnight.

"Ain't no menu, gents. Eat what everyone else does. Dinah's always surprising people with her cooking. That your dog? He's mighty well behaved."

"Not really sure," Chief answered. "He sorta adopted us. Picked him up aways back."

"It'd be a lonely world without dogs for company. The reason a dog has so many friends is that he wags his tail instead of his tongue," she chortled.

The doorway was filled with the body of a huge man. He was tall and heavyset, with dark piercing eyes, curly blonde hair with streaks of gray, and a series of chins that cascaded over his shirt-front. His avoirdupois was immense. He cut a majestic figure.

"Man, he's one big bastard," Jack said quietly.

"Sure is," Juanita answered in a half-whisper, hiding a smile.

"Whaddya do if he comes in?"

"I say, "Howdy, Ole, here's a nice table by the window." I bring a coffee. He tosses a ten on the table. I tell him to order anything he wants."

"Been in here before?"

"Yup."

"What's your highest priced meal?"

"Five ninety-five—coffee's two bits. I know it and he knows it, so we're both happier than a pig in shit. I always end up with a nice three-eighty tip."

"Well, bring us whatever the cook's got going and another shot of water for the mutt. I noticed something that looked like a motel down the street. Is it open?"

"Sure. It's run by Large Ruby. She's probably over at the cantina sucking up a few tequilas, washing them down with cerveza."

"I take it the motel isn't too busy?"

"You got that right. Other than old Doc and a couple Basques, ain't no other folks there that I know of. Come Saturday night she'll most likely get a few wild ranch hands that'll want to sleep off their hangovers."

"Okay, thanks."

Outside, the noises from within were replaced by a lethal silence.

"Time to see about a room, Chief. I'm for calling it a night—or a day in our case. I've been driving most of the night."

"If you don't mind, I'll stick with the truck. I haven't got the price of a room."

"That's not a good idea. Besides, someone has to look after the mutt. I mean Midnight. He seems to take to you. Every time I call him mutt, he gives me a sorrowful look and droops his head."

"A bed sounds good to me, sure enough."

"It's settled. Let's go find that Ruby woman."

CHAPTER TWO

Doc slowly came back to reality, his face pressed against the cold cement floor. Saliva formed a puddle near his cheek. His sheepskin jacket was open, allowing the damp cement to attack his stomach. There was no heat in the room; the propane heater was cold as an iceberg.

His fingers probed for the almost empty mescal bottle.

"Doc Cambrensis!" a familiar voice called loudly.

A big, strong hand tugged at his arm.

"Doc, you drunken souse!"

The voice grew raspier. He tried to hold onto the bottle but the hand tugged at his arm again and the bottle rolled untethered away from his reach.

"Idiot! Drunken fool! Why has God sent me to save you? I'll never know."

There was more tugging, pulling, cussing. She was a woman with immense power, and mammaries to match.

"Doc, you'll freeze to death if you don't get your skinny ass up off that damned floor. The crux of it is, hypothermia looks like it's settling in."

He was well aware of the effects of hypothermia having witnessed it in the high country of Bolivia. The complicated medical phenomenon was changing the physiology of his body.

His body temperature had probably fallen below thirty-five degrees Centigrade: A man with his meager physique could lose consciousness within ten minutes on the concrete floor and would most likely die within thirty minutes. His aching body convinced him that he'd best make a move but he didn't seem to have the energy.

The stamp of a boot near his ear exploded like a dynamite charge.

He groaned loudly and slowly lifted his head. The boot kicked him in the ribs; the pain reverberated. A strong arm rolled him over on his back. The face of Large Ruby loomed grotesquely into view.

"Have you crawled back from the cantina to die in my motel, Doc?" She yanked roughly on his arms as she spoke.

Another horrible groan.

"Is that how you repay me for saving you from certain death? You'll leave me nothing but a rotten corpse!"

His body was moving slowly. Disengaging from the glue of his vomit.

She dragged him to the edge of the bed. "Christ, you stink!"

His breath was capable of stopping a charging buffalo.

Her words grated on his foggy brain. She heaved him up on the bed with little effort, pushing his legs up following the inert body, and jerked off his boots. Then she encased his body in blankets and turned on the heater. Cursing him some more, she crawled into the bed beside him and held her body against him until he relaxed and stopped shivering.

The throbbing headache that had taken over the space behind his eyes began to subside.

Then they slept.

*   *   *

"Jack, did you hear all that moaning and groaning last night next door?"

"Couldn't help but hear it. Sounds like it finally stopped."

There was a thunderous silence between the units now.

"You figure it's almost time for breakfast, Jack?" Chief offered hopefully as he was dressing.

"Not quite. I'm in the middle of my ritual four esses."

"Four what?"

"Esses. Shit, shave, shine and shampoo. You go on over to the café and have some coffee. Take Midnight along with you. I'll be there shortly."

"Okay, if you say so. Come on, Midnight, let's mosey."

Jack had experienced another of his weird dreams.

One thing about dreams—they don't retire.

He soared above some dark and rock-strewn place, high above snow-capped mountains. There was an ebony sky and icy stars.

Below him, seen by a pale moonlight, he saw a large flat expanse of plain. It looked deserted. Huge cracks zigzagged across it like varicose veins giving it the appearance of an unidentifiable map.

He trembled in fear.

He'd seen columns of bones sticking up into the black sky, and it was up to him to keep them from collapsing. Voices, too weak to scream, held forth in a trembling wail. Icicles cut his chest without drawing blood. There were indistinct voices. He thought he heard Mel Torme—*The Velvet Fog*.

He was being immersed in a viscous liquid. He began to surface, with Ruth's face swimming above him.

He bolted upright in bed and kept his eyes open. There was no escape from the dream. Best he stay awake and face the new day.

His eyes are still heavy with sleep as he looked at himself in the mirror while shaving—deciphering all the angles he makes when he tries to negotiate space. His image was the same height as himself but twice as broad.

Can it be a premonition? He has dreamt about his own death many times, but was never fully prepared for it. Rinsing off the lather, he felt his way to the other room. He finally makes contact with the world. His convoluted thoughts are divided between light and darkness. His life is full of mysteries.

His life is one long dream.

Reflecting on his own life he decided it was dull and sort of old fashioned. Hard work, sacrifice, courage, devotion to family—wife, nation—love of baseball, and, of course, dreams.

In earlier days he was a fair-to-middlin pitcher and strong-armed left fielder for a semi-pro, Sunday afternoon ball club.

When a family came around, it was time to stop the foolishness and get down to brass tacks. Time to hang up his spikes and store away the glove.

He never lost his love for the game of baseball, however.

When he stepped outside, a coating of hoarfrost laying on some remaining cottonwood, Gambel oak and poplar leaves, met him.

Far to the west there were traces of snow on the mountains.

Only the Chief and Midnight had been brave enough to stand outside for any length of time, admiring the new-born day. A white vapor billowed from their nostrils and mouths. Chief stomped his feet to keep his toes from freezing in his meager moccasins. The uppers of soft rabbit, the soles of a double layer of sturdy elk hide.

He'd left his boots in the room.

A lone dog howls at the crescent moon in the semi-darkness hoping for an answer, or at least an echo. Midnight ignores it and points his snout in the direction of cooking odors and ambles toward the sanctuary of the café, sneaking a peek over his shoulder to see if Chief was following. It was too cold to stop and lift his leg or to scratch at an imaginary flea.

Inhabitants not in the café were hibernating under layers of quilts in their homes. The place had withdrawn into itself from the cold. It was a nasty almost spring day. A frigid, biting breeze lifted any remaining leaves without effort.

Chief walked slightly hunched over, hands clasped behind his back, and crossed the naked womb of the small town plaza which was once festooned with bougainvillea. Winter had staked it's claim on it and now it lay barren. Midnight limped ahead gingerly on sore paws. It will be several more days before they will heal completely.

A bronze statue stood in the center of the plaza, and was not preserved from the verdigris of time; on the contrary, it continued in it's original age while only the centuries grew old around it.

As he drew closer, he could make out an inscription on the base:

Diego José de Vargas Zapata Luján Ponce de Leon y Contreras
Governor of New Mexico 1691–1696

As with many explorers from Europe between the 14th and 17th centuries, Vargas held the misconception he could cleanse the heathen indigenous peoples by bringing them into Christianity. His was considered a *Bloodless Reconquest.* He failed to realize, however, that the Pueblo Indians of the southwest weren't ready for so drastic a change, and as a result, they eventually revolted. There was a definite atmosphere of hostility and suspicion.

Among the more chauvinistic of the Hispanic descendents of the original colonists, Diego de Vargas was an exception. The coming of the Spanish to New Mexico was first and foremost a mission of civilization for him.

In 1692 he gained the submission of 23 Pueblos and had baptized 2,214 Indians. This was the crux of his endeavors as Governor. The following year was the beginning of the so-called *Pueblo Revolt,* and it left Vargas dismayed by the fact his armed troops couldn't dislodge the primitive Indians from their high mesa strongholds.

He was relieved as governor and sent back to Mexico. In 1703, he managed to have himself appointed once more as governor and returned to New Mexico only to fall ill in a battle against the Apaches and died at the age of sixty.

*   *   *

The almost baroque-like style of the café was steaming with an inviting heat. The front window was fogged up from the several bodies hunkered down at a table near it with half-frozen fingers hugging mugs of coffee. Some still wore work gloves. Those that were up and about in the village, out of necessity, were telling lies to cohorts through chapped lips, not expecting an answering jibe. To help them start the day properly, Dinah was building large, spicy burritos, along with refried beans.

There were also beef steaks for those awake enough to chew them. Breakfast of the day.

CHAPTER THREE

Doc opened a crusted eye and felt ashamed as he watched Large Ruby cleaning up the mess he'd made during his rampage. A broken chair—legs smashed—a torn curtain, broken bottles. She scrubbed the foul smelling floor and washed the bedding.

She handed him a steaming cup of strong chicory coffee, laced with brandy. He drank it without a question. He hadn't spoken a word since he had awakened, his head feeling swollen to twice it's size, his whole body aching as though run over by a freight train.

"You would have probably died of pneumonia or something as bad if I hadn't shown up," she said, and waved a talon-like finger in his face. "You're actually disgraceful!" she growled, and then smiled openly.

"Why do you put up with me, Large Woman?" he managed through swollen lips.

She had an answer, but it wasn't appropriate to the occasion.

Doc had become an observer of a world he no longer lived in, although he moved through it. A muted world. Clouded. Like squinting at a painting in a dim hallway.

Large Ruby knew things about Doc's past that weren't common knowledge around the community. She knew, for instance, that Doc wasn't a physician. His degrees were in Ancient History and Archaeology. They were good degrees. Both PhD's in fact.

He also inhaled languages as though they were oxygen. French, Italian, German, Spanish and even a smattering of Basque, which he was challenging himself to learn from the Bengolarrea twins Andoni and Edur, hired on as helpers at the dig.

Andoni claimed he was a year older than Edur, having been born at 12:59 on December 31st, whereas his brother was born two minutes after midnight on 1 January.

Ruby was also aware that no less than three times Doc's slender body had been violated by the proboscis of an Anopheles mosquito.

In stages, malaria, once caught, caused cold chills, then heat, and finally sweat. If it reached the liver death could occur. By using a quinine prophylaxis, administered in a goblet of wine, he managed to thwart the stupefying abuses of the dreaded malaria.

All this was happening while he was on sabbatical in Bolivia.

Ruby once asked him what he missed most when he was down in South America. His immediate response was evergreen trees. Everything down there seemed to have huge leaves. He missed the evergreens and their needles.

He was relaxing in a small café in the town of Apolo, an isolated jungle town, some 130 miles northeast of Charazani, when he met a British biologist who invited him to join a trek to the Lake Titicaca area. The decision wasn't one of the most logical he had ever made. The journey was a grueling duel with jungle, mountains and horrible weather.

It seems this fellow was searching for Cinchona trees, the bark of which is the febrifuge of choice for treating malaria. The bark to eventually be made into the priceless quinine. They were to collect seeds from the Cinchona to be sent to nurseries in India, and the resulting plants to eventually be sent to plantations.

India was in the throes of several major diseases such as cholera, dysentery, and, of course, malaria. The East India Company was striving to control the known aspects of these problems, but were losing the battle against malaria, simply because they were ignorant of the horticulture necessary for proper growing of the trees.

Even today Doc would carry several capsules of quinine as a defense against malaria. When he first arrived at the ancient Estancia he'd noticed a ciénega—swampy area—a mile or so south of town, said to be the cause of a deadly miasma, according to the locals. Doc was much too wise to be taking any foolish chances.

Large Ruby was of Slavic extraction—or Germanic—or? With all her mass, she was yet as lithe as a ballerina in her movements. Her face was harshly painted and she swooped around the room muttering his name and humming a ditty a cappella.

She came softly to his side, bending to whisper words in his ear he couldn't comprehend. Her silky locks brushed like finest spun gold against his cheek.

Pleasure sparked and he reached for her, only to pull back, ashamed of his wanton feelings in this indecorous moment. Large Ruby's blue eyes laughed in childish happiness and her aroma enveloped him with such an ecstasy he thought he might die.

*   *   *

Jack found Chief and Midnight scrunched down near the Franklin stove. Both leveled leery eyes on him.

Chief had removed the well-worn remnants of his serape, beneath which he wore a clean, blue work shirt, and faded khaki trousers, hitched up with a tooled leather belt with a sterling silver buckle inlaid with turquoise.

Everything meant nothing to him—nothing meant anything.

"What took you so long, Jack? We about gave up on having any kind of chow."

"You look like you could do with a bit of abstaining, old man, but the dog could use a pound or two on those ribs. Let's get up to a table and see what Dinah's cooking."

Chief scanned the room from beneath his beat up Stetson.

"Appears she's got burritos and refried beans on the menu. I see a couple steaks too."

"Sounds good to me," Jack mouthed. "Best we order up something for that black killer dog too."

Midnight yawned and whacked his tail on the floor.

"Now that you've more-or-less adopted me, Jack, let's get a bit more formal. Like I said, I ain't no Chief. Full name's Cameron Yellow Fox

Arnfinn. My mother seemed to have an affinity for the actor Cameron Mitchell, saying he was just the cutest thing! Those that know me, tagged me Timco, for whatever reason. What about you, Jack?"

"My back name is Collins, but you can call me Jack."

"Suits me fine," Timco replied, as a lady slid two mugs of steaming coffee onto the table.

"You fellas gonna order or just sit there taking up room? I'm Juanita, your overly friendly host."

Jack presented a half-mouth grin. "Better make it three rations, Juanita. Our furry friend here is about to starve to death."

"Can do, but I'll have to feed him out back. Customers might not like the idea of sharing eating space with a dog."

"He won't mind, just so's he gets a full ration," Timco chimed in.

Jack asked Juanita who the strangely dressed woman was, sitting in the back.

"That be Naomi. She runs a sorta social club in those shabby adobes out west aways. Some kinda business woman, that one is. She can lay claim to that place for all I care. Her yard belongs to Gila monsters, scorpions, prairie dogs and rattlers.

"Naomi is considered a match maker. You bet! She was running a cat house long before either of us saw daylight from the depths of the womb.

She was known to sell hallucinogenic pomades to her clients in an effort to entice them into spending more cash. Her clients would make love as if engaged in joyous battle then leave in the morning quite sedate, and much lighter in the wallet."

Naomi's house of pleasure was the site of considerable uproarious carousing, however, she had a strict rule that her clients weren't to go into town to raise hell, and it kept everyone happy. She was an unbelievable woman. She wore a well-worn T-shirt with the words, *Shake Well Before Using,* stenciled across the front.

Naomi would tell Juanita, with a rictus grin, "A woman without a touch of bitchery is like milk without vitamin-D."

"Some say she's absolutely corrupt," Juanita continued. "I'll agree to that. She was fully corrupted in her mother's belly. I don't care what they say about her though. Something good can be said about everyone. You just have to spit it out."

She puckered her lips to demonstrate.

"There are people around here who like horses, others like mescal, and some even like other people. Some are customers, some work around town, and some are just plain bored."

She allowed a quick look around the room.

"I say, live and let live. Who's to judge, anyhow?"

Jack put his elbows on the table, clasped his hands together, and rested his chin on the resulting platform.

"That's one fine analogy for a gal who runs a café in this god-forsaken hole in the ground."

"Probably is, but you see I've had a bit of schoolin'. You shouldn't judge folks by their appearance, Jack. Matter of fact, I took you for a hobo or something. Running around with an Indian and a half-dead dog."

Juanita had attended finishing school back east, which was to provide her with deportment and social graces. She thought the students were all a bunch of hoity-toity snobs and she didn't need all that crap. Off she went, back to the Estancia, without a word to the headmistress.

"Touché, Juanita. Anyhow, the three of us will be sticking around here for awhile. Now, how about some grub—that is, if you can pry Dinah away from the clutches of Naomi."

"No sooner said than done. I'll take Midnight out back and serve him a full ration. Hey! Dinah!" she hallooed. "Shake your buns and rattle up some food for these two, yeh?"

When their food arrived, several flies buzzed through the swirls of blue smoke and settled on forks and the rims of glasses. Apparently they escaped the amber fly strips hung curled overhead. Several flies had already stuck to them. Jack counted a dozen, and two were still twirling their legs in an attempt to escape.

Timco jumped up from the table, a strange look on his face.

"What's up, Timco? You look like you've seen a ghost," Jack asked.

"Something ran into my leg just now. I thought it might be a rat or something."

Juanita heard the chair scrape across the floor as Timco left it, and smiled.

"You've been welcomed by the resident cat, Timco. He's only good for murdering mice. He'll take off for the kitchen now that you've been baptized."

"Maybe you should have warned me you had a wild creature in here. Scared the pee outta me. A damned cat! I hate cats! Hope he doesn't have rabies or something."

"Aw, don't get your pants in an uproar. He'll visit with Dinah now. Anyone with a can opener is of devotional interest to tha cat."

*   *   *

Dinah was taking another short break from kitchen chores and sat chatting with Naomi. She appeared to be twelve months pregnant and had to sit a distance from the table. It seems a soldier from Fort Huachuca, over Arizona way, stayed at the motel while he was in the area hunting javelinas.

Dinah and the soldier became intimate.

She was merely a receptacle for his sperm. An incubator, of sorts. He wanted to have a child, but wasn't about to be tied down with a wife. After he returned to base,

Dinah tried to contact him—without success—and announce the fact she was pregnant.

She asked Large Ruby what name he'd signed in with.

Ruby answered, "Qwerty."

Very clever. The first six letters on the top line of a typewriter. Easy to remember. Easy to forget.

Now Dinah was on the verge of becoming a single parent and stuck in her job at the café. Not such a bad thing. She could make a meal out of anything eatable, and with her country living brains, managed to do almost everything a man could.

It was skimpy consolation.

Chapter Four

Large Ruby owned a fenced-in quarter section where she kept seven domesticated mustangs, two Morgans—one chestnut, the other a bay—a Cayuse, and two mules.

Her small herd of mustangs were mostly of Andalusian and Arabian ancestry which were eventually bred into Apaloosa's by horse-breeding Indian tribes many years ago. These horses replaced the dog as a travois puller and greatly improved success in battles, trade and buffalo hunts.

Her two mules were both sorrels, as a result of the breeding jack. She would often rent out the mules as working animals as they were preferable to horses under heavy loads and showed less impatience. Doc often rode one out to the diggings rather than jeopardize his vehicle over the rough terrain.

Ruby had hired a young boy—Alfredo—who was inventing himself as an adult, to feed and water the animals and maintain the fence line. He acted like an equerry, swollen with pride, taking his chores seriously.

Since the horses and mules defecated at will, Dinah would manage to sneak a meal to Alfredo every once in awhile, if he would take a gunny sack and spade to collect the droppings. She would have him dry them out back of the café, then pulverize the mess, add water, and spread the mixture on her garden.

Once a week the boy would take his .22 rifle outside the town limits and hunt jackrabbits. He would sell them to the café and they would show up on Dinah's menu as chicken enchiladas.

Dinah's ancient, toothless pearl diver was ordered to defenestrate the dishwater after each meal to add to her lush garden. The soap had a tendency to break up the unyielding soil and also discourage grubs and such.

CHAPTER FIVE

The ostentatious cover of smooth asphalt ended abruptly at the western edge of the community. From that point—almost to infinity—it was a washboard of gravel and deep ruts. A challenge for man, beast or vehicle.

Beneath a large cottonwood, near Naomi's compound, several pieces of road equipment were parked, as though in a mobile junkyard. A heavy coating of red dust covered the aging yellow paint in an almost tessellated fashion.

When the uranium mine closed down in the nearby foothills, the County's portion of matching funds were cut off and work on the road ceased. The State wasn't too excited about continuing the road project either after losing the tax base from the mine.

There were three large ranches to the west of the Estancia al Cabo, but they didn't require a paved road since each had their own airstrips and only used the road when transporting cattle or crops to market.

*   *   *

Jack was composing letters to Maria-Rosa and Charley Briscoe at the hacienda in Texas, and another to Harry and Celeste in Baton Rouge.

He felt somewhat embarrassed that there was such a long gap between contacts.

"Hey, Timco, why don't you take Midnight out for a stroll and when I finish these letters we can wander over to the cantina to see what the social hour holds in store."

"That would be a fine idea. You know, of course, that I'm a devout radish Indian. Red on the outside, but white at heart. So, I'm certain they will not give me too much trouble in the cantina."

Regardless of his ethnicity it was hard to imagine he was half Native American. He could be taken for any number of European descendants.

Timco still maintained a white-wall haircut out of habit from his Corps days .

Jack smiled discreetly.

They entered the cantina through bat-wing doors. A young man was banging away on the upright piano, chasing dust motes with his fervor. A cigarillo dangled from his lips, the ash threatening to drop onto the keyboard.

A small Chinese person bowed to them and led them to a table, his queue trailing behind like a horse's braided tail.

"Welcome, welcome, my new friends," he announced effusively. "I am Han Po, the proud owner of this fine establishment."

"Nice to meet you. My name's Jack and my partner here is Timco."

"May I join you in a beer to introduce you to my hospitality?"

"Sure, that's fine by me," Jack replied. "Order up three and we'll clink bottles."

Han Po creased a brow in thought.

"Ahhh. But I thought it was illegal for Indians to drink."

"That may be true in some States, my new friend, but you see I'm only half Indian," Timco explained. "Half savage if you prefer. If you haven't noticed, Han Po, I'm a blue-eyed Navajo. I have a full-blooded Norwegian as a father."

"Ah, so. That's okay. There's no law hereabouts anyhow. Let's snap the caps off these bottles and celebrate. Ganbei!" He poured his beer into a Mason jar.

"Cheers!" Jack and Timco chorused.

Timco farted softly, laying a green fog over the table. "It was the wish of the wind god," he smiled.

"Shame on him," Jack said, tongue in cheek.

"Say now, that skinny little Mex can really play those keys, don't you think, Jack?"

"You reckon? It sounds more like Victor Borge dueling Liberace."

"Oh, you musn't be too harsh on him," Han Po admonished. "He's the closest thing to a musician I could hire in these parts."

Then there was another round, and more cheers! And another round, and more cheers!.

The three men were enjoying each other's company.

Han Po called to a man in greasy overalls. "Mr. Dominguez, please to join us. I wish you to meet with two new-found friends."

Dominguez sauntered over.

"Meet Jack and Timco," Han Po announced.

"Howdy. I'm called Renaldo. I run the garage and smithy down yonder."

He shook Jack and Timco's hands. The caliber of his wrists were immense. Log like. The result of working the farrier end of his business, no doubt.

"Sit down and join us in a drink," Jack offered.

"I must tell you about this one," Han Po said. "He usually has a throng of fillies lined up, hanging around his neck. It has been rumored that he was circumcised with pinking shears, and the women adore it."

Renaldo shrugged at this account of his manhood as though it were expected. He wasn't what you could call an excellent specimen of manhood, at first glance. Bushy, black, unkempt hair hung down his neck, cross-eyed in one eye, with a pot belly starting to form at belt line.

"You say you operate that garage down the street. Looks like it could have been a horse barn once," Jack mentioned. "Would you have space for me to store my pickup while I'm here? You probably don't use the whole building, do you? Leaving it out at night around here wouldn't be too smart, I'd wager."

"That would be no problem at all, señor. There is an empty room behind the workshop that has a large door. I'm sure your truck will fit it nicely. How much would you be willing to pay?"

"I was thinking maybe a dollar a night. A month payable in advance."

"That would be most generous. I'll even provide a padlock. When do you wish to begin?"

"I'll be around in the morning with cash in hand."

"Bueno!"

An impromptu party was beginning to get organized. A musical group was forming near the piano—a guitar, a banjo, a harmonica and one man playing the spoons.

The cantina was taking on life. Challenging the music, customers were singing so loud it was more of a scream.

A burly man, hair slicked back with pomade, approached their table and stood under the brim of his hat, eyeballing Timco.

"Since when did you start serving redskins in here, Han Po?"

Han Po, having consumed several beers, was trawling his memory for something to say. Something tangible. "Actually he's a front man for some Norwegian investors who're thinking of starting up a lutefisk operation in town, to be called Uff-Da."

"The hell, you say! I still don't like it, and I'm damned well going to do something about it!" He balled up his fist and made to clobber Timco.

Timco looked like a can of beer that had been shaken hard, then opened. He popped up from his chair ready for battle. He had a storm in his dark blue eyes.

"You act like the dominant male of a wolf pack," he growled. "Go ahead. Take a swing at me. But if your fist touches my nose, that's where my good nature ends."

"Mr. Comacho, I think you've had enough. It might be a good thing if you left," Han Po urged in a diplomatic way. He thought, perhaps, that Timco had a hidden stiletto, and if confirmed, would have sent Comacho to a prompt surgical death.

Jack now stood shoulder to shoulder with Timco, giving Comacho something to ponder. Two against one wasn't very good odds. They were both rather large. He lowered his fist and stalked out the door, looking as relentless as a guided missile.

"You looked like you could have scalped that idiot," Jack said.

"I never killed a man, except in battle, but I've read many obits with pleasure," Timco stated with a smirk.

A beautiful young Chinese girl, wearing a brocade *cheong sam,* approached across the deucedly littered floor, displaying a vast substantial smile and considerable thigh. She managed to negotiate the crowd without tipping her tray.

"Han Po, I have to give you credit for having the most gorgeous waitress this side of Albuquerque," Timco exclaimed.

"Ah, but she is my number four daughter, Wei, and too young to have a memory of poor times. At six or seven she was one of the very quiet ones who still wasn't used to being born.

"You see, I left my teaching job in Burbank and we moved here to get away from all the prejudice and bigotry. Also, the L.A. basin is a hermetic region of stale air and you had to cut a hole through it to breathe and see anything."

"What's that stuff on her tray?" Jack asked.

"Ahhh, yes. Locally they call them *botanas,* but I prefer the Chinese, *dim sum.* They both mean appetizers or finger food."

The music stopped briefly. The patrons were hooting and clapping in appreciation. Han Po raised his Mason jar and waved the other hand.

"What's all that about, Han Po? Everyone else is clapping," Timco asked. "You act like you don't care for the entertainment."

"There's an old Chinese saying; *It's difficult to produce sound with one palm,* so I manage to show my appreciation in my own way."

"Anyhow, how come you drink your beer out of a jar?" Jack asked.

"A habit I picked up in an Irish pub in L.A.—very strange people, those Irish and quite clannish, you know. They drink their pints out of Mason jars and their pink gin in strange-looking glasses. They also attempt to sing raunchy songs. Very off-key and very loud.

"Be aware. I see Conchita heading this way," Han Po warned. "She is an alluring succubus. A body worth it's weight in gold, but very dangerous. She's a *mestizo* of Spanish and Jicarella ancestry."

She eased down next to Jack, knees apart—not by design or habit—but as though pried apart. It was apparent to him she'd been around a man. Most likely many men.

"I think you will buy me one nice wine, señor," placing her hand on his thigh.

"I think you're a brazen hussy," he managed, gritting his teeth.

"You're very rude, you know."

"Of course. That's my nature. It makes me no never-mind. I'll break down and spring for one glass of wine. Just don 't get the idea you can homestead here."

"Oh, you are most generous. And good-looking also."

Half-way through the glass of wine, hands folded demurely in her lap, Conchita announced coyly that she had to use the restroom to powder her nose.

"Why don't you take a piss while you're at it," Jack jibed.

"You're not only rude, but also crude, señor. I may not return."

"Suits me, sweets. I'm not in the mood for company anyhow."

When she left, Timco grinned widely. "You handled that very diplomatically, Jack. What do you do for an encore? You realize, of course, she was ready to haul your ashes?"

"Go to hell!" he grated in response. "I'll admit she had a body that wouldn't quit, but it was a bit gamey. Hasn't been near water for at least a month and covers it up by drowning it in a gallon of cheap perfume."

The group near the piano tuned up for another set. It was more cacophony than symphony—as though from unhappy instruments in an unruly orchestra.

Wei walked over and said something to the piano player. Amazingly the group managed to play a melody suitable as accompaniment for her. She had a voice so beautiful it could break your heart. The cantina people seemed to be mesmerized. Even the rowdies quieted down.

"You see," Han Po spoke, choking with pride. "Orientals can sometimes calm the wild beasts without having to capture and torture them like some Occidentals. I'm so proud of my little girl."

"You should be," Jack said. "She's like something out of an opera, only prettier."

"I'll second that," Timco offered.

Renaldo nodded his agreement.

Two men swaggered to their table. One was hirsute and barrel-chested. A corpulent example of humanity.

"Here we go again," [Jack thought].

Timco stood, anticipating trouble. He made eye contact with Jack, who nodded.

The second man, tall, stooped, bowed his head and told Timco to take his seat. Timco remained standing, absentmindedly pulling on his nose with a forefinger and thumb.

The hairy one stared at Han Po beneath bushy eyebrows.

"Hey there, Chink, would that be your daughter over there?"

"Yes, I am the parent of that lovely girl."

"Let me tell you something, Chink," he said. "That's not singing, it's screaming off-key, and I don't like it one bit."

His hubris was evident. He grinned foolishly.

HanPo was stunned. It wasn't the fact this person called him names, but the fact he mouthed inanities toward Wei.

"Mu` kong yi `gie!" he screeched at this rude person.

"What in hell does *that* mean?"

"Simply that you have an extremely arrogant attitude. I don't wish you to stay in my establishment any longer."

"Screw you! I'll damn well stay as long as I want! No skinny little Chink tells *me* what I can and can't do!"

Jack and Renaldo jumped up, knocking over their chairs, and stood alongside Timco as stinging flames of words blistered the tongues of Han Po and the bully.

Timco poked a finger on the chest of the tall one, and said, "I think it's best you take your partner out of here before real trouble starts."

"Didn't mean to start something. Just funnin'. Come on Raif, let's head out."

Shortly after the encounter, Jack said, "It seems like it's about motel time. Been nice talking to you guys. We'll see you around."

When he and Timco were outside, he mentioned, "That Renaldo struck me as a man who would wear his boxer shorts for three days or more before changing them."

"I must agree with your observation, Jack. You read people very well. He could pass for the armpit of society, that's for sure."

CHAPTER SIX

The dense texture of night wore thin and the cries of a lone rooster swirled above the roofs as the sky opened slightly to allow a new day an opening. When the rooster crowed, the sun began to rise—so—the crowing caused the sun to rise.

Large Ruby gave Jack permission to have a hot plate in the room so that he could percolate coffee. It was her secret concession.

"Just don't burn the place down around me," she warned. "And don't advertise the fact that I've given you latitude."

"No sweat, Ruby. I'll be very cautious. Just like the building was my own," he promised.

He made his coffee early and quietly so's not to disturb Timco. The aroma wafted through the unit, causing Midnight to open one eye, stretch languidly and yawn. Perceiving nothing out of the ordinary, he immediately returned to his sleep.

Timco's bed creaked and writhed in pain as he turned over toward the wall.

A stroll through town was in order. Once off the main street's macadam, everything was dirt and gravel; the back streets and alleys and on out to the purlieus of the foreboding environs.

Dry and uninviting.

He guessed there hadn't been any measurable rain here for several years.

A brown membrane of sand hung like a veil over the valley partially obscuring the sun; the result of a sirocco-like wind.

Daylight slowly enveloped the town, casting copper sparkles on the mostly adobe buildings guarding both sides of the street.

There were no sounds from the sleeping adobe huts. His shadow spread a dark double of himself on the gravel.

Jack was walking an alley behind some houses when he noticed the lower half of a lady, her legs covered slightly in denim short-shorts, at a clothesline grappling with a sheet, helplessly attempting to outwit the wind.

"Need some help?" he asked, hoping for a negative reply.

"What a stupid question! Does buffalo shit stick to your shoes?"

"Guess that answers my question," he said and reached for a corner of the sheet.

A brassiere hung next to the sheet, looking like two mini-parachutes.

When they had five clothespins holding the sheet in place, Jack edged around his end and was startled to see she was topless, with a suggestion of a smile or smirk or scowl at the corners of her mouth.

"Better close your mouth before it fills with bugs." she warned.

He felt an immediate kinesthesia pull at his groin.

"You kinda caught me by surprise, lady. Not that I mind, of course. You're really quite beautiful."

"Well, thanks—I guess."

She displayed a lugubrious scowl. A quick self-evaluation confirmed her body was indeed worthy of appreciation. She thought the same of her soul, which she wasn't sure was as beautiful as her body.

"And thanks for the help. I almost lost the damned thing to the wind. The weather round here is really shitty."

"My pleasure. You shouldn't cuss so much, you know. It only helps when you're actually mad, not just peeved."

"What are you? Some kinda preacher?"

"Nah. I just like my women to be more ….like a woman."

"You're a little nutty, you know. Hell, come on in and we'll have a cuppa java, okay?"

"Sure. Why not."

The hinges on the screen door creaked.

He entered cautiously behind the lady. It was dim inside with the odor of leather and an almost fruity cuisine. The room they entered seemed to be the living room. Beyond he could see a bedroom, a small cooking area and a door leading to what he figured would be the toilet. Several old travel posters were hung on the walls. Her furniture was of rattan, sagging with age.

"I like your place. Who decorated it, the trash man?"

She pivoted, and glared. Ferociously. If she had a gun she would have shot him on the spot.

He held up both hands in a defensive position. "Only kidding. It's really a very nice, lived in room."

She relaxed slightly.

"Have a seat," she offered, "and light up if you have them."

"By the way, err ....my name's Jack."

"Oh, sorry. Forgot my manners. I'm Agnes."

She brought an enameled coffee pot and set it on a trivet on the table. Two mugs were then added.

Their hands were on the small table, a hair's breadth separating them. They sat quietly sipping coffee.

The only movement in the room was their breathing, although Agnes's was more noticeable because it lifted her breasts.

A minute or so passed by. They sipped from their mugs.

Suddenly she rose and went to a corner of the room where a diaphanous blouse hung on a clothes tree. It failed to cover much of the nakedness.

"I noticed you staring and thought I'd better cover up."

"Was I that obvious? Sorry, force of habit."

"Quite all right. It's been awhile since there's been a man around here, and I get a bit reckless."

"Oh?"

"Yup. My old man died from uranium poisoning. Worked the mine as a Super for eight years and dust finally got him. The radio-active dust has an expotential decay. The so-called experts said it would normally be excreted during digestion, but about five-percent is absorbed in the blood. After entering the bloodstream it tends to stay for many years in bone tissue. Greatest health risk is toxic damage to the kidneys."

"What a helluva way to go," Jack sympathized.

"Anyhow, the government nailed the mine owners for several infractions and gave them a time limit to solve them.

"The cheap-ass owners couldn't see upgrading. They determined it would be difficult to remediate. They'd already skimmed the best ore. They shut down. They took everything with them; money, breeze, bread knife, afternoon thunder—love. The owners failed to consider a usufruct statement to the government, and as a result, there's always some idiot poking around up there.

"There's only a handful of unmarried men left in town since the mine closed, and they're content to roam around with their zippers open.

"The many mine accidents over the years spread an atavistic attitude over the town and turned many of the widows into a solitary, horny community. The result being numerous children being born out of wedlock.

"Although many of the widow women resorted to dildos and masturbation, they mainly wanted a *real* man not some imitation or substitute. Some women even resorted to taking on female lovers."

There was no immediate reaction from Jack, so she continued.

"If you run across Eva Maurer, as you're apt to, sooner or later, you'll hear some choice gossip about the mores around here."

'You seem to know a whole lot about the mine operations."

"I should. Me and a bunch of other wives got together and tried suing the bastards, but you know how that goes. Money talks and bullshit walks. Not enough fire-power for us to hire a decent lawyer. Geez, I've been going on for ages."

Jack's thumb touched Agnes's little finger and slid over the top. Then their palms met.

Time slowed down.

With elbows resting on the table, their faces were but a few inches apart.

"Whoa, Nellie! We're getting a little ahead of ourselves, don't you think?" Jack asked.

"You're probably right. Let's wait a day or so," she grinned.

"I'm serious."

"So am I."

"Okay. How about we meet at the café for a bit of dinner?"

"Sounds good to me. What time?"

"Say about seven."

"I'll be there with bells on."

"Yeh, but make sure you wear some clothes too, huh?"

"Smart ass."

He left Agnes in a light-hearted mood, in anticipation of their next meeting.

He wandered down the alley a short distance, and soon intersected one of the gravel roads. It was seemingly deserted with the exception of a group of cackling chickens. Nocturnal gales had carried them from their coop. Someone left the door unlatched.

The air grew dense with a potent egg smell seconds before lightning split the sky. He ducked into a doorway just as the bolt struck the building. The inside walls were blackened; several ollas and other items were untouched, however, a copper kettle hanging over the cooking fire area was melted into liquid.

Parts of his clothes and the hair on his head and arms were singed. The door he had just entered was torn from it's hinges and the frame split asunder.

The sand outside the doorway became vitrified.

To make matters worse, he pissed himself from fright and it ran in rivulets down both legs. If he'd been a female it would seem as though the amniotic sac had burst.

He recovered sufficiently to search his body for any possible permanent damage. The trauma was enough to make a believer out of him. Not so drastic as to send him to church though.

He stumbled out the gaping hole that had been the doorway and grabbed at the course adobe to steady himself, bruising his hand.

Jack had become an agnostic. He had his religious doubts. At one time, in his youth, he was an altar boy. He even enjoyed Catholicism. The Sunday Mass, confession, the Rosary. It had all been fun.

He even considered Maryknoll and priesthood. Reading history—modern and ancient—changed his way of thinking.

Later in life he started bypassing mass and confession, eventually only to attend church at Christmas and Easter simply to appease his wife, Ruth.

Now he had religious doubts and found no guilt in the fact that the only religion he now had was sitting beneath a towering cathedral-like tree watching a cloud ride the sky.

He considered nuclear power and weapons as anti-Christ elements. He would have nightmarish visions of orange and white mushroom clouds hovering over a densely populated city with the people screaming for God to help them.

It was absolute insanity.

After a few deep breaths, and shaking his arms to see if they worked, he headed back to the main drag and steered his body towards the western edge of town, seeking the garage/blacksmith shop. He wouldn't go back on his word with Renaldo to stable his truck and pay the rent this morning.

He found Renaldo deeply engrossed in conversation with a person in the dark confines at the rear. He appeared to be in priest's garb.

Renaldo caught a glimpse of him and stepped in his direction, with a hand signal to warn off his conspiratorial cohort, who slipped out the back door.

"I'm not interrupting anything important between you and the priest, am I?" Jack queried.

Renaldo glared. "What priest would that be, señor? You know, sometimes a statement like that can get a person in a heap of trouble. I don't think you really saw anyone, now did you?"

"So. You can always use the four letter word."

"And what would that be?"

"Stop."

"Anyway," continued, "you look like a pile of crap this morning."

"Probably do. Came near getting zapped by lightning. Helluva thing. Not a cloud in the sky. No thunder either."

"Ah, yes. You've got to realize, Señor, that in the desert things are different. I read somewhere that the blue-white explosions of positive lightning can originate from a cumulonimbus cloud several miles away—without warning."

"I'll try to remember that. Anyhow, here's your payment for storing my truck. I'll bring it around this afternoon, if that's okay with you."

"Bueno. I shall expect you."

Jack made his way back to the motel for a quick shower and a change into dry clothes.

Chapter Seven

The café was almost empty. Timco was leaning back in his chair conversing with a man dressed in a chambray shirt and well-worn jeans.

'Hey, Jack! Join us! This here's Doc."

"Hi Doc. Nice to meet you."

He offered a hand and found the man's grip strong and his smile warm.

Both men eyed him suspiciously as he joined them at the table.

"Guess I'd better explain my appearance," Jack offered.

He proceeded to expose his encounter with the lightning.

"Geez, Jack! You're one lucky sonnabitch!" Timco said, astounded.

"I suppose you're right. Could have been a lot worse," he agreed, nervously biting on a corner of his lip.

Juanita placed a platter of food in front of Doc. It was piled high with three eggs over easy, hash browns, a rasher of bacon and three pieces of toast. He dropped a dollop of salsa in the center of two eggs giving them the appearance of bloodshot eyes.

"You gonna eat all that, Doc?"

"Sure as shootin'. I've been off solid food for three days, and the body told me to stoke up on some vitamins. I'm sure you're aware that it was me raising Cain last night. I go on one of those toots every once in awhile."

"Sorta figured it might be you," Timco acknowledged. "I heard Ruby yellin'—very loud, I might add."

Timco fidgeted a bit before announcing to Jack, "I've been offered a job out at Doc's digs, and since I'm without funds, figured it might work out just fine. I was going to spring it on you, but things happened too fast."

Doc eased himself further down in his chair, and waited for the outburst that was sure to come. "I don't mean to break up your friendship, Jack, but I really need some help out there, and most of my crew will be a bunch of young people. Timco can be sort of a buffer, so I won't have to worry too much."

"What kinda digs we talking about, Doc?"

"I've been commissioned as an archaeologist to uncover a long-lost pueblo, working in conjunction with the museum and university. The site's about a two hour's ride southeast of here."

He waved a piece of toast in the general direction.

He mouthed a large portion of his meal and continued talking, chewing rapidly as though someone might make off with some.

"Timco said he'd help me set up camp for the workers due in from New Mexico Institute of Mining and Technology. He'll also act as on-site guard."

"Sounds like quite a project to me," Jack said. "How long do you suppose all that's going to take?"

"Hard to say. A lot depends on the weather and also what kind of workers they send me."

He pushed the empty plate away and burped loudly. "That's the sign of good manners in Japan. It shows you enjoyed the meal and the company at table," he said seriously.

"And after a good lay—," Timco lifted a leg and farted.

They both folded over and laughed with gusto.

The beginning of a friendly relationship.

While the three men were talking a two and a half ton, four-wheel drive truck pulled up in front, a fully loaded trailer behind. *Workman Diversified* was painted on the door .Juanita bustled about moving a table and some chairs as the door swung open. She was making room for her acquisitions, all the while humming.

"Cliff! It's good to see you amigo. Did you bring them?"

"That I did, my love. Bring me a coffee and let me catch my breath. I'll have them in here in jig time. Good to see you, Doc. I've got all your stuff out there too. The whole kit and caboodle."

Cliff had finessed Juanita into bringing a pin-ball machine and a one-armed bandit to the café. Strictly on the QT, of course. Gambling was obviously prohibited in the county.

Cliff was a real piece of work.

His Jacobian nose preceded him to a chair at an empty table.

He was pale, and like a Mormon, he wore a white, short-sleeved shirt and a narrow tie. His chin appeared to have crumbled away like an outcrop from a chalky cliff. He had watery eyes that were constantly alert, searching side to side, checking everything in sight, missing nothing, as though expecting the law to pounce on him in an instant. His eyes were shaded by a black, beat-up straw ranch hat that belied any thoughts of pleasantness from the owner.

Cliff is a chameleon as to his religious beliefs—an assimilated Jew only to the point of being Mormon. He was like a chameleon changing his politics, religions and language on a whim, depending on the situation.

He was also a confirmed prankster.

There were those that knew him intimately. He was famous for being a tight-wad and overly stingy, not withstanding his somewhat clandestine overly generous ways. A label placed on him by gentile associates.

Cliff was a predator in many ways. He was aware that his skin would prickle at the nape of his neck when the wrong person was behind him. He didn't wish to be bothered with trivial matters during most of the day. Those hours were for business only. He was most active during crepuscular periods.

All in all, a sad-looking excuse of manhood. Other than the fact he practiced Judaism periodically, he could be considered to be a *Jack Mormon* as he imbibed caffeine and beer with gusto and smoked nasty smelling black cheroots.

He was subject to violent oscillations between attraction

and aversion that those of his ilk suffer as entrepreneurs. Customers would lean very close to him, listening for the slightest shift in his sales spiel, hoping to take advantage of a verbal slip of the tongue. It wasn't so much to humiliate him as it was to seek a business advantage.

The insecure position of Jews in the west, socially, in business and within themselves, should explain why they think they own only what they hold in their hands or what they can earn easily, through craftiness and guile.

It was much safer back east among friends and family.

"Notice he's got those pointy little ears. Sorta like a bat. He's got the face of a falcon; the frame of a crane," Juanita expounded quietly to the uninitiated at the table. She actually enjoyed having him around.

Once the two machines were installed, it gave the café the appearance of a mini-casino.

Dinah heard the ruckus out front and rushed from the kitchen. She was fascinated with the slot machine. A beautiful piece of equipment. Flashing lights and all. It wouldn't pay off in coins, of course. Just free games. It made little difference.

"I need something to occupy my mind besides sex—which isn't all that bad, you know," she announced to no one in particular.

"Okay, Doc, if you're finished eating, want to ride out with me and help to unload some of your stuff? I could use these two hefty sorts too. What say, gents?"

"Fine by me." Jack answered. "So long as I'm back here in time for dinner. I've got sort of a date."

"Well, la-de-da!" Timco chortled. "Getting a bit perky in your old age, huh?"

"Not really. Just someone I met today."

"All right, guys, let's git to gittin," Cliff urged. "I have a couple more stops to make later."

CHAPTER EIGHT

As he climbed into the truck, Jack motioned to a plastic bag on the seat.

"What's this stuff?"

"Before you ask, don't ask," Cliff answered. "It's matzah. Sort of like maize tortillas. I like it for snacks. Better for you than eating sweet shit."

"I'm not in the habit of eating shit," Jack growled behind clenched teeth.

"Try it some time. Guano's the best." Cliff said with a lazy curling smile and sardonic eyes.

"Yeh, and you're so full of it your eyes are turning brown. You remind me of a sheeny rag picker going around town in a cart drawn by a horse with a straw hat perched on it's head with holes cut for it's ears."

Cliff shrugged off the comment. He was used to those barbs. Besides, he knew exactly what Jack was referring to.

Jack tossed the bag into the glove compartment.

The trip out to the digs was, if nothing else, gut wrenching.

The air was quiet after the death of the slight breeze, and dust plumed up behind them in heavy clouds. Everything was still.

Cliff was a cautious driver and managed to miss one or two ruts and a like amount of rocks out of the thousands they encountered along the route. They veered southeast, circling around several small mesas, and bypassing numerous arroyos.

Small ponds, formed after periodic rain storms were scattered hither and yon. Around these ponds were rings of white salt, poisoning the soil, left behind as the water rapidly evaporated under the burning sun.

They forded the Deception River. It wasn't much of a river, as rivers go, but it was a year-round source of the precious commodity, water. As unimpressive as it was, it provided life to crops and cattle along it's course. It was easily crossed on horseback or waded by foot in some places.

It was narrow and sluggish, crawling through the wild hinterland without a care in the world.

They were soon in an immense canyon, some two miles wide and almost ten miles in length. The walls were of sedimentary sandstone and rose to a dizzying 200 feet.

Unlike most igneous and metamorphic rocks, the strata contained fossils, the remains of ancient plants and animals.

Wind, sand and water from flash flooding over millions of years are the primary weathering agents of sandstone and often produce amazing structures.

Rock formations that are primarily sandstone usually allow percolation of water and are porous enough to store large quantities, making them valuable aquifers.

Fine-grained aquifers, such as sandstones, are more apt to filter out pollutants from the surface than are rocks with cracks and crevices, such as limestones or other rocks fractured by seismic activity.

Colors will usually be tan or yellow, from a blend of clear quartz and dark amber feldspar. In the southwestern United States additional colorant is iron oxide, which gives the rock reddish tints ranging from pink to dark red. Some manganese will tint a purple hue.

The sandstone in this canyon was a result of sedimentation,

compacted by years of pressure from the overlying sea and resulting in the layers of various colors.

*   *   *

When Doc first arrived in the area, he was quickly given a lesson in subsistence economy, when he found he couldn't buy eggs locally. People hereabouts only had enough for their immediate families. Everything in the land was either food, fuel or building material.

Surrounded by the harsh environment, locals adapted and eked out a living.

Timco would have it much easier with a full larder provided by the expedition backers.

Cliff removed his tie and reached behind the seat for a pair of jeans. He then swapped patent leather shoes for work boots.

The unloading went off without a hitch. Now scattered around the site were the makings of a modified 20 by 48 foot Quonset hut—to be used as a workshop/office, living space for Doc and Timco, and kitchen, two chemical outhouses, a large 10 by 20 foot mess tent, and six 2-man tents for the crew.

Doc's personal tent had been set up on a slight incline adjacent to where the Quonset hut was to be erected. Timco now had exclusive use of it, albeit temporarily.

Twenty 5-gallon jugs of potable water and all the victuals to carry the crew for several weeks were to be stowed in the Quonset hut after assembly. It would be Timco's job to remain on site to erect the mess tent and commence building the Quonset, which was a marvel of engineering. It was designed to be assembled without skilled labor. Theirs would be placed directly on the ground with a wooden floor.

Not that there was any immediate threat of pillagers, his collateral duty would be to guard the stores and material.

When the truck, towing it's naked trailer arrived back at the café, Cliff took Doc aside and explained that he would haul the generator, four 55-gallon drums of fuel, ten gallons of oil and a new battery out to the site in a day or so. He needed to capture a fork-lift for the heavy items.

"That'll suit me just fine," Doc said. "I don't expect my crew will be showing up until at least the week-end."

Doc had an adequate contingency fund and worked a deal with Juanita to lease the generator.

The diesel generator now sat idle behind the café where it had hibernated for the better part of five years. At one time it was the sole provider of power for the few buildings wired up.

Electricity was furnished several hours each day when it ran; growling and puffing black smoke and emitting noxious fumes. Usability was controlled by the café's hours—usually from near sunrise to seven at night. It was very expensive to run and maintain.

Now tall electric towers, like undressed hussars in formation, strode across the landscape, providing power around the clock with a flick of a switch.

Chapter Nine

Agnes was kerplunking coins into the one-armed bandit as fast as it could swallow them up. A glazed look in her eyes and part of a gleeful smile on her lips.

"Agnes!" Jack called. "Come here! Eat! Your food's going to get cold."

She enjoyed pulling the handle more than she liked the possibility of coins dropping, which was unlikely. The winning games added up slowly. The wheels stopped whirling abruptly. She was out of coins and free games.

"What are we having, Jack? It smells fantastic!"

"Dinah did herself proud. Stuffed pork chops, potatoes au gratin and a crisp salad, straight from her garden out back."

"Yummy. I'm famished!"

"What's with the dress tonight?" he asked.

"Just thought I'd like it instead of jeans. I haven't been on a real date for ages."

"Good deal. I like it. Makes you look like a teen-ager, but the more you try to be like someone else, you'll find *yourself* standing in the way," he scolded, and looked away.

And so.

It was silently agreed upon. There would be no need for conversation for the next several minutes while they devoured the repast. It wasn't time for prating. It was time to savor the meal, the company, the evening.

When the food had been consumed, Agnes raised one eyebrow and asked, "Do you think my house is burning down?"

"I don't know," he answered with a sly grin. "Let's go check."

*   *   *

Jack figured Agnes would be the last person on earth he expected to make love to, but he knew they were going to make love. It was simply a matter of waiting for it to happen.

As she fumbled to open the door, he pressed her against the wall. They kissed, open-mouthed, with tangled tongues. She could feel him pushing his member against her belly through clothes and all.

They were still kissing when they entered the house and began stripping off their clothes. They fell onto the bed and were conjoined immediately. They fit together like a well-tuned engine.

The room was dark. Agnes reached over him to light a candle. Everything was blurred—the illumination wasn't worth the effort.

"Jack! I recognize you!"

She laughed merrily.

"Yup, it's me alright. You seem to be awfully horny tonight."

"Almost every night," she replied coyly. "You're a horrid man, you know."

"Not so"

They locked eyes.

They made love again.

"You're a horrid man, you know," she repeated.

"You're the one who seduced *me!*"

They lay quietly for several minutes, taking turns smoking a cigarette.

"Well, Agnes, you sure surprised me, that's for sure."

"Why so?"

"I'm not really sure. Can't put my finger on it."

She felt him tense up and almost physically repel her.

It wasn't love. It couldn't be love. It was almost fear. A fear of becoming attached. He wasn't ready for all this. There was a certain riddle involved.

"Is everything all right, Jack? Is it something I've said or done?"

"No, it's just me. Subconsciously I'm experiencing a sort of drowning, and I'm having trouble swimming. I can't explain it. I'm sorry. I'd better leave before I make a complete ass of myself and start blabbering all over you."

"Is there something—?"

"Sorry. I'm just not good company tonight. Maybe some other time?"

Very slowly she eased herself out of the bed, and stood naked, statue-like, waiting for him to dress.

Jack put life to a cigarette and blew out a cumulus formation of smoke.

His goodnight wasn't a funeral but never-the-less sad.

Not to say—is to say.

* * *

After leaving Agnes he took an alternate route back to the motel. Along the way, he stood in front of a magnificent replica of a Chinese house, topped with a pagoda-style roof.

It's gotta be Han Po's. As he stood there admiring it, a raucous shout, followed by considerable loud, agitated Mandarin was heard coming from the back yard.

Now he was certain this place belonged to Han Po, and decided to investigate, hoping he wouldn't be skewered in the process.

Han Po, dressed in flimsy pajamas, was chasing a colorful Pekin Bantam around the yard in a frenzy. When he saw Jack, he stopped long enough to catch his breath and scream, "That chicken is no good! It wakes me up early every morning and doesn't even lay me one egg. I think it goes into the pot!"

After surveying the situation, Jack said, "You don't suppose it doesn't lay eggs because it's a rooster, do you?"

"What are you?" he screeched. "Some kind of Confucius that is trying to agitate me more?"

"I'm only trying to calm you down, friend. Anyhow, if the creature did manage to lay an egg, it would take at least six of them to make a meal. Don't you agree?"

"Jack, I suppose you're absolutely right," he answered with a slight grin, giving in to logic. "That still won't make me forget the food and sleep that the feathery enemy has deprived me of."

Placing a hand on Han Po's shoulder, Jack tried appeasing him. "Take yourself inside and forget tonight. Tomorrow you'll see things in a better light. I'll meet you in the morning at the café for coffee, okay?"

"That will be most generous, Jack. Very few people will sit with me for even a short time."

"Then it's a deal. I'm off for bed. See you in the morning."

He walked off towards the motel.

A woman's voice flew out the door of a hut like a sparrow into the evening air.

A man shouted.

A dog barked.

Children cried.

The cur sidled up and mounted his leg, tongue hanging out.

"Get the hell outta here, you mangy mutt!" he growled at the dog and cuffed it alongside an ear.

*   *   *

Yellow Fox and Midnight were in the café early. He was reminiscing about some recent events. Midnight lay curled up at his feet, snoring.

"Hey man," the burly patron said. "Don't I know you? Face looks familiar."

He was a vigorous, gregarious type with close-cropped hair.

"Don't think so. Been up around Wyoming for almost three years."

"Yeh? Where at?"

"Outside Gillette. Running herds."

"Gillette, you say. A damned forest of oil rigs nowadays! Didn't know they was any cattle left around there."

Some of his words were stolen by hacking coughs as globs of phlegm smacked the floor. Midnight sent a disgusted look his way and moved to safety further under the table.

"Oh, yeh," Yellow Fox offered, trying to ignore the gross person's actions. "Them oil folks put some little fences around the derricks so's the beeves have some grazing space between them."

"How many beasties you reckon roam around up there?"

"I figure maybe four to six thousand total. There's still plenty of range around Thunder Basin for 'em," he mentioned without too much conviction.

"I'll be go to hell!" the stranger exclaimed. "Well, gotta be mosey'n. Nice seein ya agin."

"Yeh. Same here. Con cuidado."

Who in hell was *that* character?

The years were embalming him as an eternal youth.

He ordered up another cup of coffee.

In Wyoming he was on a hegira from his wife.

Before he left it seems he spent more time with an old shell-shocked Marine than he did with his wife and kids. Other than the male nurse in charge, Yellow Fox was the only other person the old man talked to. He had to be spoon-fed like a baby, and while chewing he would moan inanities and begin crying.

He'd been gassed somewhere in France in World War One. There wasn't a Veterans Administration back then and he struggled to stay alive after returning home—mostly on the streets—as there was no family to look after him. The male nurse at the County Hospital used his off-duty hours to tend him, he with the marmoreal face, the twitching around vacant eyes and the limp arms.

Then there was another dent in his long-range plans. Three years looking at the backsides of stupid cattle was more than enough for Cameron Yellow Fox Arnfinn. He'd head south before the first frost hit.

On his journey he was temporarily delayed by enrolling in courses of philology and epistemology, under the G.I. Bill, at New Mexico Highlands University in Las Vegas. Ever since his tour of duty with the Marines as a Code Talker, he'd been interested in linguistics and nature.

Yellow Fox's matriculation efforts were short-lived, however, as a Hammurabian verdict was passed down by the faculty to the effect that his attendance was marginal, at best, and it was deemed he didn't show enough aptitude toward his chosen subjects.

In a nut-shell, he was merely taking up valuable space in the classrooms which could be better utilized by more dedicated students.

Occasionally his mind would segue into personal matters, such as his wartime experiences: but not often.

The once super-secret Code Talker Project began with twenty-nine Navajos at Camp Pendleton, California. They applied Navajo words—there was no written Navajo language—to military terms. Soon there were over 300 code talkers, Yellow Fox among them, deployed to the South Pacific's island hopping campaigns, confusing the Japanese with this strange language that they couldn't decode.

Most of the code talkers were Navajos but others familiar with the language were also recruited.

Other than mingling with fellow code talkers, Yellow Fox was basically a loner. He couldn't tolerate the troops from the south, labeling them *crackers* and mimicking their talk: "Don't y'all unnerstan ennythin 'bout the *real* langige spoke aroun' heah?"

As in all military groups there was a constant bickering. Yellow Fox usually stayed aloof. He did have one non-Indian buddy who was from Brooklyn. He had a sharp name that would never get fat. His use of words totally dismayed him, and when he spoke, Yellow Fox would have to contain himself from laughing outright.

"Hey, Tonto, whatcha doin' tanite? Let's me and you pawk owa asses in de club and suck up a cuppla brewskis."

During one of the campaigns, his group plucked Corbin Shaw, an Australian coast watcher, from amongst jungle debris where he'd hidden from the enemy.

Later, Shaw dragged a wounded Yellow Fox to safety under heavy enemy fire. When they got back to their lines, Corporal Corcoran was tending his still in the trench. He concocted his *torpedo juice* using raisins and spuds. The mixture was at least 300% alcohol by volume and could peel the paint off a tank. Shaw used some on Yellow Fox's wounds until the medics arrived; eliciting a scream from the normally sedate Indian.

Yellow Fox promised himself he would visit Australia after the war and look up Shaw, but he never quite got around to it.

At cessation of hostilities in 1945, when troops were being released on a point accumulation system, the code talkers were overlooked— shunted aside—and it wasn't until early 1946 that the government, in it's infinite wisdom, finally discharged them.

Eventually, in 1968, the code talker operations were declassified and they were allowed to relate some of their experiences.

*   *   *

On the road again, he decided the more things change, the more they stay the same.

Ostracism held no boundaries.

After all, Yellow Fox knew things that were anti-transcendental and that were pantheistic in nature.

Another coffee was ordered.

On his continuing journey back to the Navajo Nation he had a destination in mind, but there was a huge void that must be overcome.

There had to be something on the other side of the sunset.

Some day all this will come to an end. What will it matter?

Wins and losses will fade from memory. It won't matter which side of the tracks you live on. Even gender and skin color will be irreverent.

Will anyone grieve after I'm gone? Who will remember me?"

From a very early age he had to interrupt his education to attend a Federal school on the *Rez*. There he was totally immersed with fluent Navajo speaking kids. His mother insisted he speak English at home. Otherwise he'd end up like those drunken bums in Gallup.

In somewhat sober, lucid moments, of which didn't happen often, she related to him stories of his grandparents, of whom he knew nothing. She enjoyed the re-telling of the *Long Walk*.

This took place starting in 1863 after the Army, with Colonel Kit

Carson in charge, decided they couldn't control the heathens of the west any longer, destroyed all their crops, burnt all the peach trees, stole all the sheep and rounded up more than 9,000 men, women and children for the 300-mile march to Fort Sumner (in an area called Bosque Redondo—*Hwééldi* by the Navajo) in the Pecos River Valley.

At least 200 died along the way.

It was a complete disaster for both sides. The place was disease ridden and rampant starvation soon took over. Crops failed soon after planting. The experiment was declared a failure, and five years later the people, called *Diné,* were allowed to return home, to their own lands.

The Long Walk would be repeated in reverse.

He wasn't *Jóhonnaá éi* (the sun bearer) but perhaps he could shed some light on his miserable lifestyle.

As a youngster he was brought up in the back seat of a Hudson Hornet, subsisting on junk food out of a grocery sack and treats, such as M&M's, from the glove compartment. The heater didn't work so he cocooned himself into an old beat-up sleeping bag. Really quite comfortable, considering the circumstances.

His mother drove like a wanton banshee and usually didn't desire to stop; whether for emergencies or calls of nature. She provided a milk carton for him to use to relieve his bladder. Worked fine if she didn't hit a chuck hole. Then it could become a messy disaster.

Saturday nights he was dropped off at the bakery—a dollar bill clutched in his hand—to out-sly the regular adult shoppers for deeply discounted bakery goods. His mother had an aggravated sweet tooth. One of the clerks would hold forth in this depression sale. The gleaners would queue up according to arrival time—never before seven p.m. in accordance with the store's policy. That would allow late shoppers priority over any remaining goods. Yellow Fox and the others would stay in their slot in the queue by unspoken agreement.

Yellow Fox was usually the first or second in line and managed to procure some well-chosen morsels for his mother. Occasionally he would be rewarded for his efforts with a glazed donut or iced cupcake if the thought entered her whiskey-addled brain.

He was also relegated to baby-sitting his younger sister after school so that his mother could earn a few dollars washing dishes in a diner and cleaning up at a motel.

One evening his mother came home to find him asleep on the ratty settee. The family cat was lying on his sister's chest. It had stolen her breath. She was dead. His mother snatched the offending animal away, and with a screech and loud cussing, tossed it across the room, bashing it's head against the wall.

She didn't say anything to Yellow Fox. Didn't blame him. Simply ignored him thenceforth.

His Norwegian father deserted the family for a tramp steamer and was lost to the world forever. He had met a fellow Norwegian, Olav Reirsen, at the Sons of Norway Hall and they took off together.

About all he inherited from his Norse father was his stature and fair skin. The remainder of his psyche was entirely Indian in nature.

And, of course, the Vikings enjoyed fish. Fish! He couldn't stand the odor of canned sardines or kippers. Dead fish, he declared.

His mother received a letter from him—once—from Tahiti, pleading for some traveling funds. She spit on the paper and threw it in the trash. The man turned his mother crazy.

Every evening she would sit solitarily in the Green Hornet chugging on her post-prandial beer.

She was finally let go as a chambermaid at the motel in Gallup and ended up selling the Hornet for food and booze money. It was all down hill from that point on.

Yellow Fox had left the confines of the Hornet when he was fourteen and went to work bucking bales and shoveling manure at the livery and hustling grade school kids out of their lunch money.

After a year of that enterprise, he became bored. The mournful sound of a train whistle led him to the switching yards in Gallup. Other than the clothes on his back and seventy-five cents in change, his worldly goods consisted of an ancient Horner harmonica.

Riding the rails was a new experience. He met many interesting people, who like himself, were seeking relief from the world's rules and regulations. In one boxcar he met an ex-banker who was disillusioned with the way the country was heading and insisted we would never break loose from the depression.

"We're going to hell in a hand basket," he would announce, lighting a tailor-made cigarette with a gold lighter.

He may have been right.

Cameron Yellow Fox met many other displaced Indians. They all spoke the same language. Destitution. After all it *was* the depression. They would hunch around a small campfire, cooking stolen potatoes, and telling outrageous lies about being misplaced warriors.

One of those warriors spoke of joining the military. He said he saw a billboard with a picture of Uncle Sam pointing and saying, "I want you!"

He swore the finger was aimed at him.

"Think about it, hanh," he said solemnly. "My grandfather was conned into taking residence on the rez first, under government control, and then during World War One ,they told him he could still be a warrior if he joined up."

Yellow Fox thought deeply on this subject. He wasn't really thinking about being a warrior, but the idea of traveling to some strange lands, away from the rez, appealed to his gypsy-like blood. Besides, there would be three *hots* and a cot, something that was lacking in his present condition.

One of the trains he hopped was loaded with Army vehicles. He managed to find an unlocked truck and crawled into the cab. He rode this marvelous machine all the way through Arizona, feeling as though he were driving it. When the train stopped to add an extra engine to haul it over the pass, he jumped out and began hitch-hiking back home, to—what?

At sixteen he lied his way into the Marines. He dropped a brochure of the Marines on the kitchen table and announced, "I'm gonna join up."

All his mother had to say was, "The hell you say!"

He had become quite adept at forging his mother's signature on excuses for absenteeism from school.

In boot camp he discovered the whites were still pissed off over the massacre of Custer. If one of his buddies in the Indian platoon screwed up, the entire platoon was relegated to *dive bombing* the compound. This consisted of patrolling the area with a broom handle that had a large nail imbedded in the end. The object was to spear discarded paper objects and cigarette butts and dispose of them into a burlap sack which was slung over the shoulder with a wide strap.

A heroic assignment.

Another choice detail was the planting of bulbs and flowers in front of the General's home. This was considerably more fun than dive bombing. If one were to visit the area a month or so later, there would be nothing but a well spaded flower bed, and brown debris. The troops were pulling the roots off each planting as it was inserted into the soil.

After boot camp he was assigned to the Code Talker Corps platoon.

The code talkers were an elite, top secret unit, recruited from the Navajo Nation during World War II, to provide rapid transmissions of vital information during battle. They used the Navajo language to transmit military information which completely confused the Japanese code breakers. Their Indian code was never broken.

Ironically, they were often mistaken for the enemy and came close to death by our own Marines. It took diplomacy to keep them alive and eventually they were assigned a white Marine to escort them everywhere.

During the Okinawa campaign, Yellow Fox was wounded twice more, receiving the Purple Heart with two bronze stars for his injuries, and was also awarded the Bronze Star for bravery. As with many of his cohorts, he didn't accumulate enough points to be discharged at cessation of hostilities and it wasn't until early 1946 that he finally received his orders.

When he returned home he was always seen to be fully clothed—even on the hottest days—covered, protected against the elements, as opposed to being defenseless as a naked person. It was a camouflage, preventing prying eyes from observing his scars of battle.

His contention was the only heroes were dead ones, and he didn't wish to be placed in that category.

He realized he would stand out among nudists.

Soon after returning to the rez, he was approached by one of the elder diné to take part in a Curative Ceremony. These ceremonies are designed to purify the Navajo from all the evils they had witnessed on the outside of the rez and to blot out memories of what had happened during the war.

Many code talkers returned with souvenirs taken from Japanese victims, such as bayonets, bits of uniforms, and objects found in pockets. Probably a throw-back from the days warriors took scalps to show their bravery.

The items were buried in the ground and shot at four times with a rifle, cutting off all communication between the Navajo and his enemy. By this act he was brought back into harmony with nature.

Yellow Fox felt cleansed after the ceremony, however, he was wont to move around freely now after his Marine Corps stint, and decided to do some traveling. The rez was now too confining. There was small opportunity available so he set his sights on other endeavors besides basket weaving and conning the tourists.

His mind returned to the café. His hand slithered across the table like a tentacle of a frustrated octopus, in search of the handle to his coffee mug.

At that precise moment, blonde, green-eyed Milo *Doc* Cambrensis, the displaced Welshman, took it upon himself to join him. In the process of taking a seat, he managed to squash the south-end two inches of Midnight's tail. It produced an indignant yip and a scurry for safer territory beyond the table's confines.

"Sorry," Milo mouthed to the injured animal.

His reverie interrupted, Yellow Fox scowled at Doc.

"Besides bothering me no end, waddya want, Doc? Can't you see I'm contemplating immense things?"

His semi-paraplegic hand, still groping for the coffee mug, managed to knock over the salt shaker—the top coming off—manufacturing a mini snowdrift on the table's surface.

"That tears it Doc! See what you've made me do? Juanita's going to throw a tizzy, that's for sure."

Doc ignored the outburst. "It seems I have a slight problem, Yellow Fox. Now that most of the equipment and material has been delivered to the digs, there's a distinct possibility it may be pilfered without someone to guard it. Do you suppose it would be possible for you to get out there today?"

Yellow Fox laid a finger alongside his nose and glanced off, a frown creasing his brow.

After a long pause he said," Now just how in hell do you propose me getting out there, boss? Damned if shank's mare will make it. And, besides, we haven't talked salary yet."

Doc wrote a figure on a napkin and shoved it across the table.

"Fine. That'll suit me. I'll take along Midnight for company and grab some take-out chow from Dinah to hold me over until I can set up camp."

"Agreed then. I'll meet you around noon with a horse and pay for the victuals you'll be taking. By the way, Yellow Fox, you don't seem to be married , am I correct?"

"Haven't been for quite some time. The woman left me when I took off for Wyoming. We had two kids. My wish was for the children of my loins to grow tall and straight and intelligent. I realized the best thing I could do for them was to love their mother. I accomplished that with a passion, but it didn't seem to make much difference. She wanted stability. Ran off with a damned dentist! I tried everything to make a go of it. the only thing I didn't try was suicide."

"That's a shame," Doc replied without too much feeling. "The reason I asked is the digs might take some time to finish and I wouldn't want to mess up your home life."

Yellow Fox shrugged. "No chance of that happening. I'll stick it out."

"Excellent."

They shook hands and parted.

CHAPTER TEN

Yellow Fox sat astraddle of a camp stool in front of a recently erected tent, the nadir of his spine barely resting on the canvas seat.

His coffee mug sat on an upturned packing crate. He was studying a rough diagram of the camp arrangement laid out on a piece of quad paper.

Peripherally he caught movement to his left. Midnight's hackle raised and a low growl escaped from deep within.

"Easy boy."

Three horsemen approached slowly and dismounted.

"Howdy," the scrawny one said through the side of his mouth. "Just wonderin' what's goin' on here. Seems to be a helluva lot of activity."

"Nothing special. Just a little surveying for Indian stuff."

"Looks like a big deal to me. There's enough gear here to start up a town."

They were slowly fanning out.

Yellow Fox had his back to the sun and had them at a disadvantage. His tethered horse began staling and then whinnied, temporarily distracting them.

This didn't appear to be a social call.

"Maybe a small town," he answered. "I'm here alone as you can see."

The grubby one on the left displayed a large gap between his front teeth when he grinned.

The third man of the group hesitated slightly and rubbed the trace of the white scar between his nose and upper lip—the outline of his cleft palate.

All these traits were mentally recorded by Yellow Fox within ten seconds of their arrival.

With his left hand he reached for his coffee mug, drawing their eyes in that direction. He slid his right hand slowly to his boot top and drew a sweep-tip knife from it's sheath, the surgical steel of which held the fine edge similar to a Toledo blade. It glinted menacingly and curved into a grin as he palmed the elk antler handle.

Grubby decided to make a move.

He was too slow. Yellow Fox was on him in a flash, threatening to slash his throat.

The apparent leader of the trio waved off the scrawny one who was reaching for a saddle carbine.

"Leave them be, Raif. What we have here is some kinda fag being whipped on by an insane aborigine."

Yellow Fox glared at the other two riders. "I'd suggest you all high-tail out of here before I get serious and start skinning you alive. I haven't had any fresh meat today, and y'all look mighty tempting."

Another low growl from Midnight.

"Ah ,hell, fellas, ain't nothing here we might be needin'. Let's leave this hombre with his flea-bitten mutt and head on out," the leader whined.

He turned to Yellow Fox and said, "Bravery and stupidity are close allies, you bet! Only the results separate them."

He winked as he mounted and swung the horse's head away from camp.

CHAPTER ELEVEN

Ruby espied Jack walking off toward the café as the telephone jingled. She put two digits in her mouth and whistled loudly.

"Hey, Jack! Telephone for you!"

He entered the office and she handed the instrument over.

"Hello? Hell, Harry, I'd almost forgotten I wrote you. How's it going and where did you find this number?"

"Jack, mon ami, the stationary you appropriated had the telephone number of the motel on it, but no address. I noticed a post-mark of New Mexico and figured you were some place around there."

"There isn't any address, Harry, just *here* is good enough. They use a P.O. box and mail's delivered on a rural route."

"Celeste and myself have had a concern for you. We haven't heard from you since you were in Texas. Are you alright?"

"Never better."

He grinned across at Ruby.

"Some really great country around here. This part of New Mexico has me hypnotized. By the way, if you two aren't tied down, want to come out for awhile? Fishing's not the best, but you can try for black bass in the almost dried up river."

He paused for a second. Getting no reply he continued.

"I'm getting ready to help a guy who's digging on an ancient pueblo."

"Now, that sounds interesting, for sure. If we come out do we need to bring our own shovels?"

"Hell no! We've got all the tools you'll need. I also have enough spinning gear for both of you, so leave all that behind. If you decide to come, I'll make arrangements at this end to have you picked up in Albuquerque."

"That sounds good, my friend. Celeste is out shopping but she'll be overjoyed to hear you're sort of settled once again. By the way, she won a jackpot on one of the river boats and can't wait to put it to use."

"Good for her! I'm sure that between us we can figure a way to lighten her wallet, eh?"

"Yes indeed. By the way, is there a name to that place?"

"Sorta. It's a town built around an old Estancia. Called al Cabo. Not on the map though."

"Ah, yes. Very picturesque, I would imagine. I'm sure Celeste will want to share it with you."

"Picturesque? Not hardly. But I guess you could call it that for want of a better description."

He smiled into the telephone and Ruby joined him from across the desk. She was catching snippets of the conversation.

"Anyhow, Harry, let me know when I can expect you and I'll have things ready."

"Bon. If you don't happen to be around, I'll leave a message with that sweet-sounding lady who answered the telephone."

"She might be sweet sounding on the telephone, but she can clean your clock if you try anything funny."

"I wouldn't plan on anything stupid like that with Celeste around. She'd slit my throat while I'm asleep. Haaa! I'll say adieu for now. Expect to hear from us soon."

Click. The connection was severed.

"I assume a friend of yours?", Ruby asked.

"Very good friend. Harry and Celeste will probably be coming out for a visit. They're from Louisiana. You'll like them."

"That's great! New blood always livens up the place."

"I'll pay for their room."

"Sure you will. But no discount."

"I wouldn't have it any other way, Ruby. Business is business. Speaking of which, can I peek at your motel register? I want to play good guy. See if I can trace down that soldier that pumped up Dinah."

"Hey, now, that's a fine idea. Have at it."

There was a good chance he could locate Dinah's paramour. He was in luck. The rental car's license plate was listed. Now he could contact the rental company in Sierra Vista and con them out of a name.

"Thanks a bunch, Ruby. Now I'll play like Sam Spade."

*   *   *

Jack started for the café. Ruby called after him to wait up.

"I'll join you, if you don't mind. I get damned tired of drinking my coffee solo."

"Hey, you don't have to ask, you know. I'm always willing to join a lovely woman over a meal."

"I've got ulterior motives today. I think Doc is over there and I want to see if he's half-way sober. He'll be heading out to the digs tomorrow and I want to see him before he goes."

"I'm sure I saw him wander in that direction earlier," Jack mentioned casually, not wanting to get involved with their romance. They make an effort to keep it under wraps, but most of the town is aware anyhow. Those two should get married.

Doc was hunched over a bowl of beef/barley soup; a dish of salsa guacamole and crackers nearby.

"Howdy, Doc, mind if we join you?" Jack asked.

"Can't see any way to avoid it. I see you brought along the woman."

"You're very observant. By the way, this woman, as you call her, is Ruby, who I think you already know."

"Sorta. Is there something you wanted, or are you two just out bar hopping?"

Doc's attitude wasn't a wanton hubris but rather pride in his accomplishments. As with many intellectuals he was probably overly-educated and lacking any shadenfruede towards more common individuals. It wasn't as though he felt superior, but impatience was just under the surface and could almost be considered one of his virtues.

"Well, professor, if I may call you that, I wanted to ask you to take a small bundle of personal items out to Yellow Fox when you go tomorrow," Jack asked sarcastically.

Doc laid his soup spoon down precisely at a ninety-degree angle to the bowl.

"I suppose that wouldn't be too much of an imposition on me. After all, he's my on-site guardian and I should attempt to appease him, don't you think?"

"Get off your high horse, Doc, and make believe some of us minions do our best to satisfy you," Ruby interjected.

"Oh, I suppose that's meant to rile me. I just happen to have feelings for my fellow man, but apparently they're hidden beneath the veneer. Certainly I'll haul those items out. There was never a question."

"Then I imagine you'll be wanting to use one of the mules?" Ruby asked.

"As a matter of fact, yes. That ancient Volvo of mine can't take too many more trips across that unforgiving terrain before it becomes a piece of debris."

Jack sat on the rustic bench outside the café enjoying a post-prandial cigarette.

Ruby went across to the motel with intentions of taking a bath and relaxing for awhile on her small balcony overlooking the square.

Doc followed a few minutes later. She stood on the top of the stairs in a flowing robe which gave her the appearance of a huge bat about to take off in flight.

She remained landlocked.

It wasn't time for man to fly unaided.

"Why don't you come up for a minute, Doc? I'll fix you a nice cool drink."

"Very well. I suppose for a short time. I have to arrange things for tomorrow."

He entered her apartment and immediately began opening windows.

"What the hell do you think you're doing, Doc?"

"Getting some air. This place smells."

He took a seat near one of the open windows. A glass jar stood on the sill with an avocado seed—propped with three toothpicks—was immersed part-way in water. It would be the start of a new tree.

"Just what you need, Ruby. Something else to baby-sit."

Ruby rustled about in the kitchenette and managed to locate the makings of a drink. She brought it over to Doc and grinned. She caught him looking raptly at her.

"Why are you staring at me that way? I think you have a mild priapism," she said, eyeballing his crotch.

"That's the best kind."

"Well, don't," she said smiling. "I have other things in mind for tonight."

"Okay, then, slip into something *less* comfortable so I don't have to sit here and ogle your half-naked body. I'm not really looking at you, I'm beholding you."

"First of all, nothing's going to happen between us. Not tonight, at least. I'll be stuck in this hell-hole with nothing to do but twiddle my thumbs."

"I'll try to get into town at least once a week, unless something drastic comes up. Well, maybe every other week."

"See what I mean? You're as about reliable as the sun coming up in the west. I'm going to get out of this outfit and insist you take me over to the cantina for a farewell drink. Don't say a word. Just accept it."

He wanted to go tomorrow with the absolute knowledge of how lovely she was to him. That was all.

"We're not going to have sex tonight," she said.

He couldn't agree more.

"I can't agree more," he mumbled.

"Okay, then. Let's play alligator and drag ass outta here before it gets mushy."

*   *   *

They found Jack and Han Po in deep conversation, chuckling every so often. They seemed to enjoy each other's company.

"Doc, grab another chair from that table and order up some drinks," Ruby ordered in an officiating manner.

"I might, and I might not. Who made you the big kahuna? All of a sudden I'm supposed to be your slave? I don't think so," he groused.

"Oh, take It easy. You can be a real shit sometimes. Don't you have the slightest bit of a sense of humor?"

Chollo sat with his compadres across the room. He ran a complete oligarchy, including the three mescalaros sitting with him.

"Observe, my amigos, the señor over there sitting with the gorgeous, large woman. He is one intelligente hombre. You will notice he only drinks Añejo, and then nothing but *Dos Gusanos,* with the two worms. I have seen him devour the gusano rojos—red worms—once the bottle has been emptied."

"I have, myself eaten the gusano rojo at uno restaurante in Jalisco," Arturo Comacho announced proudly.

"Si. That may be so, but you will notice the one raised eyebrow. It could possibly mean he's questioning.

"The slight half-mouth grin.

"The finger alongside his nose.

"These things set him aside as a man of breeding."

"But what does all this have to do with us?" Tony Luna asked, swilling down his beer.

Chollo twirled the ends of his Mischa Auer-type mustache. Taking his time before answering.

"You can actually read this man like a torn page out of a book. Hah!"

Tony was quite impressed. His leader certainly was a smart man.

"You are a very clever person, Chollo."

"Si. I know. These things mean nothing at present, but soon we shall put them to work against him and his gringo friends out at the pueblo. He has no idea we are not ignorant about this activity. I have already dispatched three men to investigate the strange workings out there."

*   *   *

Estelle, the waitress, made an abrupt entrance and began a sequidilla to the accompaniment of her castanets. She twirled around the small dance floor like a whirlwind, flipping her voluminous skirt into the faces of several patrons, taunting them.

Her high-stepping prancing caused Han Po some consternation. The two by twelve inch floorboards were sturdy enough, but the old foundation was in peril of loosing it's grip on terra firma.

"Does she put on this act often?" Jack asked.

"Only when the mood takes her," Han Po answered. "It causes the men's mouths to dry up from cheering and they order more whiskey and beer. This makes my abacus to work overtime. It is mutually beneficial. She manages to collect immense tips."

Estelle finished her impromptu floor show and plopped down on a customer's lap, smiling seductively, waving a hand in a circle to order a round.

"Seems like another good evening for you, Han Po. The cash register is singing a real nice tune," Jack observed.

"Yes. We have one of these good nights every once in awhile. *Bai zhé bu` náo*. It is written : to remain unshaken despite a hundred setbacks."

"You always seem to come up with some crazy explanation, don't you?" Jack asked.

"It is the way of Chinese idioms. There is always a proper explanation for everything. You *must* agree."

A grubby-looking cowboy patron stood on his chair and announced loudly that he could out-drink anyone in this here friggin joint, and proceeded to chug-a-lug a pitcher of beer, chasing it down with a double shot of red-eye. Whereupon he puked all over the table, the chair, his boots and anything else within striking distance.

Han Po was unfazed. "He certainly wasted a good evening. I'll have the swamper clean up the mess and toss him out back to sober up. Excuse me for one minute."

Evidently Estelle took it upon herself to plop down on the wrong lap. Having searched for her husband for over an hour, a very irate wife stormed into the cantina, espied Estelle on her hubby's lap, and tore into her with no mercy.

They grappled for several minutes, seeking an advantage, clawing, tearing hair, cussing and generally raising a hullabaloo.

A wicked right hook sent the wife sprawling. Estelle had the upper hand, and was now sitting on the wife's back. She reached up to the table and took a drink of flat lees.

Han Po thought she might be refueling—preparing for the next onslaught. She squinted up through one eye twisted with smoke.

"How's that for an encore, folks? No applause necessary. I'm going to let up this hot-tempered bitch now so she can lead her old man home by the nose.

"Anyone for buying me a fresh glass of wine?"

There were many takers. None of whom would end up taking the wild woman home.

"Is that the end of the floorshow for tonight?" Doc asked. "Nostalgia isn't what it used to be," he added, with a rictus smile, gazing through his pale gray-green eyes behind rimless glasses.

In the meantime, Agnes made an appearance and cozied up with Jack. One hand reached under the table and made contact with his crotch. He immediately produced an erection as hard as a railroad spike.

This brought a smile to both their faces.

Agnes would take him home.

Console him.

Relieve the tension.

It was the proper thing to do.

"Folks, I'm going to leave now. Seems Agnes needs an escort home," Jack said with a slight bit of embarrassment.

"No need to make excuses, Jack. If the place wasn't so busy, I might have the same idea," Han Po chuckled, "and use some root."

Han Po was referring, of course, to the adaptogens and aphrodisiacs; nourishing stimulants of red ginseng, which supposedly prevent sexual dysfunction in men.

Certain laboratory studies found that some forms of ginseng enhance the libido and copulative performance.

CHAPTER TWELVE

"How long do you expect to be out at the digs, Doc?" Ruby asked.

"Hell, woman, I haven't the slightest clue. I'll know better when the team shows up and we start excavating the site."

Ruby displayed an enigmatic smile with a fire in her gaze.

"Oh hell. I guess I *could* ride out every once in awhile. To be ignored there would only be half as bad as not having you around here."

"I wouldn't put it so harshly, Large. I expect we can take turns coming into town once in awhile to refresh bodies and replenish supplies. After all, this is an amazing find and it will take our full concentration to document it."

"I suppose you're right, as usual, Doc, but—."

"Right or wrong is good, but then there's the middle ground," he said. "I'm not real sure how you feel about us Ruby, and I'm a bit slow on the draw. Probably why I'm still single at forty-five."

"You do alright for yourself, Doc. I wouldn't get too concerned. After all, you've got *me* under your spell."

"That's me in a nutshell. I'm ensnarled in punctilio towards you."

"What's that in plain English?"

"It simply means I've got too much couth to think about ravishing you."

"Now, that's the sweetest thing anyone's ever said to me, Doc. And you didn't even crack a smile."

*   *   *

There was a message for Jack on the answering machine. A representative from the AA Rental Car Agency in Sierra Vista, Arizona was trying to make contact.

Jack dialed the number and waited for a response.

"Hello there. I'm calling to find out who rented a car from you. It seems the motel owes him a rebate and we're trying to locate him. He was a soldier from Fort Huachuca. I've got the license number of the vehicle, if that will help."

"Certainly, sir. Let me check our records."

Jack grinned. *This is going to be easier than I thought.*

"Yes. Here it is. The name is Corporal Peter Anderson. I hope this will be enough for you, sir. Company policy forbids me to divulge anything else."

"That's just fine. I'll take it from there. Thanks again. So long."

Jack dialed the operator and asked for the number for the Fort. It was connected immediately and he asked for the Locator's Office.

"I'm searching for a Corporal Peter Anderson. He stayed at our motel awhile ago and we find that we owe him a rebate. Would it be possible for you to contact him and have him call me back?"

"We'll do what we can, sir. Leave me your name and number where we can reach you."

An hour slid by at a snail's pace. He thumbed through a six-month old magazine.

He was munching on some peanut brittle from a jar on the desk, compliments of Ruby, when the telephone came to life.

"Hello. This is Corporal Anderson. I understand you need to get hold of me."

"Hi there, Corporal. My name is Jack Collins and I'm calling from the Rainbow Motel. Remember it? You stayed here on a hunting trip recently."

"Uh, yeh, I remember the place."

"Well, Pete. May I call you Pete?"

"Sure."

"It seems that while you were here you met a young lady named Dinah at the café and became, shall we say, involved. Nature took over and your seed was planted. She's now quite pregnant."

He paused for effect.

"I'm just acting as a good Samaritan, you understand, and I'd like to see you do right by her."

"Well, geez, Mr. Collins, I don't really think I can afford a wife and kid. It was a good roll in the hay, but that's all we figured on—both of us."

"Okay, I can understand that. I've got an offer for you. Just listen for a minute before hanging up. I have the means to help you both out. If I paid your way back up here, and set up a descent wedding, would you go along with it?"

"Christ! I'd have to think about that. I sure wouldn't want Dinah to raise the kid all by herself. I'll ask my Captain if I can take off for a few days. I've got some leave time on the books so that won't be a big deal. How about I call you back tomorrow?"

"Good enough. I'm sure you'll make the right decision."

*　　*　　*

Jack needed a few items from his pickup and headed over to the garage after breakfast. The board and batten building was actually a four-stall horse barn: four stalls on the left with a large workshop and two additional rooms on the right. Renaldo, or his part-time mechanic didn't seem to be around, so he went directly to his rented room.

He began sorting clothing and a few personal items.

There was a subdued cabal of voices filtering through the wall of the adjacent room. Once his small bundle was cinched, he walked over to the wall and listened intently.

He recognized Renaldo's voice, but the others were muffled; indistinguishable.

A large knothole was nearby. He peered through it and managed to make out four figures. There was Renaldo, the one he thought to be the priest, and two others. They were talking and gesturing toward several plastic-wrapped packages lying on a makeshift table.

He was now damned certain the person Renaldo was talking to before was the priest person, who now stood a mere six-feet from him. It was obvious they had been plotting. Waiting for the other two.

Bridles, bits and hackamores hung from pegs. Along the opposite wall were cheekpieces, browbands, nosebands reins and other paraphernalia customarily used by horsemen.

Two well-worn saddles rode sawhorses. Jack was familiar with all those items having seen them at the hacienda in Texas where he had spent some time. This surely must have been the tack room at one time.

The men stepped back a bit and Jack couldn't make out what they were saying. The words were garbled within the heavy dust motes and spider webs.

The two newcomers stepped aside. They appeared to be vaquero's. One was an unsavory looking character. The other, dressed in black from head to toe, more impressive looking; shiny boots, an elegant white shirt with ruffled cuffs, a low-slung holster on his leg.

All the finery was concealing a thin, upright body. He spoke with uvular accents.

The unsavory person raised his voice. "I'll take my share now, hombres, whether you like I or not. I'm headin' the hell outta here!"

"Where'd you park your horse?" Renaldo asked, with a sneer.

"Gave him a whoa and ground-hitched him out back."

"I reckon you had this all figgered out before, huh? I think I'll rip that crappy hat right off your dumb-ass head," Renaldo threatened. "I'll wager you won't get too far with that spavined animal you own."

"I'll take my chances."

The vaquero reached behind his neck to grasp a sheathed knife slung there.

He grabbed one of the parcels and made for the back door.

"Leave him be," the priest grumbled. "He ain't getting far."

The three remaining cohorts pulled back a loose board and began stashing the items inside the opening of the wall.

Jack had seen and heard enough. He walked around to the front of the truck, and without thinking, shut the door loudly.

"What in hell is that! Did you hear it?"

"Sounded like that dude with his truck in the next room."

"Get your ass over there and find out how much he knows, growled the priest to the slick-looking vaquero.

Jack was just leaving the barn when the man confronted him.

"Hey, Anglo, whatcha doin?"

"Just getting some things from my truck. Why?"

"Oh, nothin'. Have you seen anything strange around here?"

"Nope. Just some dumb horse out back farting up a storm."

"Yo! That'll be my amigo's. He's leaving soon."

"Right. Well, I'll be heading back to the motel and sort this stuff out. See ya around."

"Si. We'll meet again, señor."

He nodded slightly and smiled. Dumb gringo.

He spotted Chollo down the street. "Hey, Chollo! Come here! I have a small job for you."

"What is it you require? I'm on my way to the cantina to relieve this poor, dry throat of mine."

"Nothing you can't handle. My compadre just rode out and is heading southwest. I wish for him to meet with an accident of some permanence."

He pursed his lips and squinted, as though considering how much he should divulge.

"He will be carrying a small parcel that we in the barn wish to have back. Can you handle that?"

"I think so, amigo."

"I'm inspired with confidence," the vaquero sneered.

"It is but a simple request. I can track him down shortly, but first, a cerveza."

"Very well. Don't take so long that we will become anxious and might possibly think you're backing down."

"Have no fear, amigo. I shall report back long before sunset with your prize."

"Bueno. You will receive some solace in the fact there will be a generous reward."

Much before sunset Chollo presented himself at the barn. The smirking bandito announced he was nominating himself as a —partner in their potentially lucrative enterprise.

"The unfortunate hombre is now buried up to his neck and covered with *melaza.* The fire ants will have a glorious feast, starting with his eyes.

His own eyes flashed impishly.

"The coyote opened the parcel to check it's contents. Seems he removed a small bit for his own use. You can see that most of the goods are still inside. I now find it more beneficial to become one of the insiders rather than to merely get a bonus."

"Well, now," Renaldo asked. "Do you think, perhaps, you might be chewing off more than you can swallow?"

"Oh no! You see, I have many contacts that we can use as mules. They are most discreet and will welcome some extra pesos rattling around in their pockets."

"Very well. You can join us on a trial basis. When you have proven yourself and those mules of yours can produce, we'll consider making you a full partner. Is that agreed?"

"Si. You will not regret it."

"I have faith that you'll honor your word and do good by us," Renaldo said to his back as he left.

He glanced at the priest. They had a silent conversation.

A nod, a wink, a slight raising of an eyebrow. There was always the chance Chollo might be an asset—but then again—he might have to be disposed with in some manner.

"Do you really believe that cock and bull story?" the priest asked.

"What do *you* really believe?" Renaldo countered.

"I don't give a rat's ass. He'll get his comeuppance soon enough, you can bet on it!"

"That's not very Christian, my imitation priest. Have no fear, amigo. A liar needs a good memory and he'll slip up sooner or later," Renaldo said with a smirk. "Anyhow, I trust him as far as a horse can throw it's own dung."

CHAPTER THIRTEEN

Timco, along with Midnight, was in town for some R&R. The student workers could handle things in camp.

Jack woke up wringing wet. Another dream—or was it a nightmare?

He was on the verge of a magnificent discovery. There was an ancient man blocking his way. His eyes had the egg-white cloudiness of an old dog. He had a strange shape to his head. It was tumescent and didn't fit the size of his body.

The discovery had to be held in abeyance as he was becoming dizzy and would fall from the chair shortly. He feels certain pleasure on being relieved from his duties of living. He was confined to a very small space. He had agoraphobia and felt quite safe.

He raises himself up on the chair to see a length of rope dangling from a beam. The smoke from his cigarette rises slowly and makes his eyes smart. There would be only a few moments for him to form a noose and encircle his neck with it. There would be no more pain, no more worry. It would be a long sleep.

He woke with a jolt.

His sleep had fled and would have to be hunted down in the other side of the room. He pulled the straight-back chair away from it's site beneath the small desk and moved it near the window. Morpheus had been defeated once again.

He stared with crusty eyes into the darkness—the world outside seemed friendly enough.

He daydreamed about his youth. Snagging frogs at Duerney's pond, picking blackberries in an empty field, eating wild onions— washed down with the juice of crab apples— playing mumblety peg with his father's jackknife, writing his name in the snow with piss—never could dot the i—much to his chagrin. The sign on the outhouse wall at Boy Scout camp: *For the health and sanitation of camp Curtis S. Reed, please close the lid.* Chewing pitch from some kinda forlorn excuse for a conifer or a glob of tar that had bubbled up from the road in the heat. These were the closest he came to actual chewing gum.

Timco woke to the smell of Jack's cigarette.

"Jack, why do you insist on torturing yourself? Your wife's been gone for how many years now? There's still a bunch of like left for you to live. You seem to have an obsession with thoughts of death. I suggest you turn them off. Think more of pleasant things. Dream of pleasure."

Timco was always apprised of Jack's dreams.

"I know. You're probably right, as usual."

He dressed slowly and quietly and told Midnight to follow. "Let's sneak over to the café and grab an early breakfast."

A slight whine, but he acquiesced and went to the door, tail agitating the air.

He sat perusing a letter from Charley Briscoe. Ruby slipped the envelope under the door last night.

The patriarch of the huge Texas landholding, Maria-Rosa Herrara, had passed away silently in her sleep. A slight smile on her lips and a peaceful mien about her, even in the long rest.

Charley apologized for not replying to Jack's letter sooner, but he had been overwhelmed with details concerning the *Casa de Aqua Delgada* and it's accompanying 275,000 hectares. He was now the beneficiary of the sprawling operation as was specified in Maria-Rosa's will.

Jack grinned. He knew Charley would continue to run the spread as before, keeping traditions alive.

The letter ended with a profound statement that caused Jack's throat to constrict and his eyes to water slightly:

Jack, I'll always consider you my brother and also a very close friend. I still remember how you brought happiness to a lonely old woman. She mentioned you often after you left.

As a matter of fact, the whole hacienda feels the void left by you. They have nothing but good thoughts of you.

Your very good friend, Charley (the grouchy cowboy).

Chapter Fourteen

Jack entered the mercantile seeking a few supplies. He needed coffee, some sugar cubes, canned milk and something to nibble on.

Seated on the counter, legs swinging freely, sat Don's wife, Eva. She sat stoically, contemplating a peanut shell on the floor .She was dressed in a green print cotton dress, with a wide patent leather belt. Her face was the color of an old saddle with creases of worn leather. Her dark shiny hair was put up in a bun.

"Howdy, Mr. Collins. Been expecting you'd show up one of these days," Don said."

Jack handed over his short list and wandered through the shop while his order was being filled.

The shop was a veritable cornucopia. He espied a Radio Flyer hanging from a beam. The epitome of wagons in his childhood. His wagon was made from the wheels of an abandoned baby carriage, some scrap wood and determination.

Every shelf, and all the wall space, was filled to capacity. There were plumbing supplies, farm and ranch equipment, equine gear, toys, canned goods, Levi's and Wranglers, Ariat shoes, power tools and any number of other useful items and food staples.

A mini–Macy's and A&P combined.

"You've got quite a nice selection here, Don. Inventory alone must keep you on your toes."

"Sure does. keep adding things as people request them. Been here going on fifteen years now and pretty well know the wants of my customers. Even got me a freezer and 'fridge now thanks to REA coming through five years ago. Word's out and around you can get almost anything here—from iceberg lettuce to Key Lime pie. Not that I stock them, but it doesn't hurt business with the word-of-mouth advertising, you might say."

Jack neared Eva and she put out an arm as if to delay him.

"Mr. Collins, have you had a chance to see much of the town?"

"Just a little. Haven't been here all that long."

She proceeded to tell him tidbits with a sharp tongue, honed by gossip to a razor's edge.

"One thing you'll notice as you become familiar with the place is that all the young children appear to be older, more wrinkled. The babies are born old here."

She paused for effect.

"Even so, they're taught good manners. Not to poke your finger up your nose. Bending to pick up things that grown-ups have dropped, opening doors for them, and such."

A person could be overwhelmed with words from this woman. A giant tidal wave of adjectives.

News dripped from her lips like melting icicles. Her words hovered across back yards and over pigeon droppings on the church steeple.

"Let me tell you about Iris Hopkins. She's put three husbands in the ground during her forty-nine years, and also, according to her neighbors, hasn't been without a gentleman friend or two lately, unbeknownst to her current hubby.

"Just last week I saw a woman with two black eyes, and you'll hardly believe how much it altered her person for the better. She was a woman who trimmed too much of her husband's hair."

"Give Mr. Collins a break, Eva. You've been at it for a half-hour without rest." Don warned with a grimace.

It didn't faze her in the least. She continued, not skipping a beat.

Eva cherished the fact that she was the guardian of most of the town's secrets: the mystery of silence just before a secret was revealed to her. The larger the secret, the denser the quiet surrounding it. Timing was a most important factor—to choose when, if at all, she would whisper the contents of a recent secret to see if it would increase in detail as it made it's way around town. If she waited too long to divulge the latest tidbit, most of the thrill would have drained away.

Some things were better to remain secrets. There might not be anything juicy to hide for weeks on end and she would hold the key. People would come to her seeking stories, stories she told about others in their small town that was infected with a silence when a person was confronted with questions.

She knew something about almost everyone and could practically read their minds. It was as though their secrets would come to the surface like water farts in a bathtub. They called her a snoop, a pain in the ass. But they kept coming back. They wanted desperately to hear some dirt about their neighbors and relatives.

Some of the villagers called her accursed, repugnant, with a sneering sarcasm. She was privy to those plotting intrigues, once hidden, now openly obvious to her.

In reality she was tormented but couldn't quite place the cause. It was as if a demonic entity ruled over her, as if she were plunged into an element she couldn't control.

She traveled through the town with purposeful strides, shoulders thrown back like a drill sergeant, eyes fixed and cold on a potential prey. She had an animal expertise in trapping gossip. Brazen and defiant at times, but honey-tongued out of necessity in order to glean fresh information.

People were strained under her weary interrogations. It was a two-way street of choice information and she reveled in it. Her most lucrative sources considered her a gadfly—not to her face, of course—and Eva avoided calumny, outright. It didn't fit into her scheme.

Words tumbled out of her mouth, without a pause, without a trace of human warmth.

"That's all very interesting, Mrs. Maurer, but I'm not too concerned. I sorta stay to myself. I really don't have time to chat right now, so if you'll excuse me—."

She wouldn't be put off so lightly. After all, she had a multitude of tidings to pass on. She was a composite of boring subjects to Jack, and could easily act as a douche of cold water on any conversation.

Finally, without further ado, she plopped down from the counter and with an ostentatious shrug headed out the door without even a fair-thee-well or adios.

The bell above the door tingled in her wake.

"Gone off to fill in some blanks, I opine," Don said. "Sometimes she's like that Imelda Marcos twit with the thousand shoes: every time she slips into another new pair she has an orgasm, I swear. Yesterday she was in a bitchy mood—more than usual, I mean—and I hoped it was PMS and not morning sickness."

Jack smiled at this and replied, "Okay, Don, I'm outta here. How much do I owe you?"

"Not a sou. I'll put you in the ledger like everyone else. Believe it or not, I actually come out even some months."

"By the way, that clerk of yours is rifling through the magazine rack."

"Oh, you mean Martin. No problem there. He steals words, not the magazines."

"Alright then, be seein' you at pay-up time."

Chapter Fifteen

On this quiet Sunday morning in town, an air of languor, bordering on torpidity, was in evidence as shadows shrank back from the vacant street.

A complete metamorphosis.

Jack stood in the shadow of the Mercantile and watched the devout trundle towards the church. They were mostly Indians and Mexicans and probably didn't understand an iota of the gibberish inside, mainly because it was basically in English jargon. Little did they know the priest was also unaware of the sermon's teachings.

The few male whites in attendance were soon asleep in their pews, some out of necessity following a night of carousing.

Jack waited there for several minutes, contemplating the deathly quiet.

Of course!

There hadn't been any bell summoning the people. That's what was missing. He couldn't remember any church in his childhood without a bell. Sunday was like a virtual carillon of sounds—each church trying to outdo the others. They all seemed to have an altar boy or sexton, as the case may be, pulling vigorously on bell ropes.

Out of curiosity, he walked over to the entrance of the church and stood listening for a moment or two. The priest was expounding—relying on a stack of notes—on the healing powers of Saint Francis of Assisi. Jack recalled from his Catholic teachings, the association with the church, and all it's many saints, that Saint Francis was not the *Healer.*

Hazily he recalled the Healer to be Saint Brigid of Ireland. Something didn't seem right. It was obvious this priest hadn't studied hagiography to any extent or else hadn't paid attention to detail.

Father Donovan, of Jack's childhood, wouldn't have made such a faux pas. There was something almost surrealistic in the way this priest stood behind the pulpit, arms outstretched, as though beseeching the congregation to believe his blasphemous litany.

Morning mass, my ass! This poor excuse for a priest would do well to shut his mouth and just have the people pray.

It was also rather obvious he was wearing hand-me-down garb, as it was much too small for his large frame. By no stretch of the imagination were these his remnants.

The small congregation huddled closely together, fingering their rosary beads, ignoring the spiel from their Anglo priest.

Suddenly his head bobbed down behind the pulpit. He had dropped his notes, from which he couldn't proceed with the fiasco, since he was semi-illiterate in church matters and not at all familiar with the scriptures. They were entirely foreign to him. The notes were his saviour.

Then his head popped up like a yo-yo and he once more took control of the pulpit, but with a desperate look on his face. Sweat ran down his brow. The congregation didn't display the slightest bit of curiosity.

This, most likely, wasn't the first gaffe he'd made, [Jack thought]. The priest had installed himself into a world about which he was completely ignorant. Strangely, he was more Talmudic in his leanings.

The inside of the small church intrigued Jack. Age didn't seem to have had a negative impact. The highly polished wooden floor was immaculate. Overhead, massive oak beams held the roof in place. Oddly, the only religious decoration apparent to the eye was a large oil painting of the Virgin Mary on one wall. There was a door behind the pulpit, most likely opening to the priest's chambers.

He strolled around the thick-walled, 400 year-old adobe structure. Attached to the north wall was a small, one-room schoolhouse, the ilk of which resembled the one in *Little House on the Prairie,* by Laura Ingalls Wilder. He always enjoyed that show.

There was an ancient well out back; two cows snacking on sparse brome grass. A pear tree was espaliered against the south wall. What would happen to it if the wall suddenly crumbled, as it might eventually?

A child stood nearby tending his burro.

"Do you know who Jesus is?" he asked him, wondering if he had been taught in the Sunday school.

"Si. He is the wooden statue on the wall of my mother's house," he answered proudly.

"Fair enough. Here's a coin for you to spend foolishly."

"Gracias. I have a good plan for it's use, señor," he replied with a low bow and a sweep of his battered sombrero.

The sunshine was suddenly turned off as an immense dark cloud invaded the sky.

CHAPTER SIXTEEN

The morning was beginning in a gentle manner.

Most activity on Saturday took place at night in the cantina. Jack was enjoying his breakfast of biscuits and gravy when Cliff sauntered in.

"Where's your yarmaluke, Jew boy?"

"Stuffed in my pocket, if you must know! Only wear it when I attend synagogue in the city, and you make me crazy, Jack Collins!"

"And you make me meshugganah, Cliff Workman. You're a hard person to read."

"From what do you know meshugganah?"

"From the kosher-eating smucks in Bronxville who always tried to spiff me until I threatened to slap them alongside the head with a pork chop."

"Anyhow, this ain't no synagogue," Cliff whined.

"Maybe not, but God's going to punish you, you wayward kike!"

"If you insist on calling me sheeny and kike, I'll be forced to call *you* a black Irish mick."

They enjoyed taunting each other in the east coast vernacular.

"Call me whatever you want, just so it doesn't interfere with our relationship. By the way, Cliff, I've got a couple friends coming tomorrow for a visit. What'll you charge me to have Ernie pick them up in Albuquerque?"

"I'll let you off easy, Catholic puke. Hourly wages for Ernie, plus gas."

Cliff was, if nothing else, a vainglorious person, and his feelings were easily hurt.

"Good deal. I'll let you know what time their plane gets in."

Cliff's driver, Ernie, once ran a cesspool cleaning business back in Indiana, but the effluvial odors finally caught up with him and he decided to head out west, hoping to find some air he could breathe without agitating his sinuses.

Cliff called him a dork. He still insisted on wearing Oshkosh b'Gosh bib overalls; nothing civilized like Levi's.

*   *   *

The café was taking on life. A very large, dark and handsome Indian sat alone near the rear, dressed in the shirt of the Tribal Police and wearing jeans and boots.

He was stationed in Crownpoint, one of the seven districts that comprised the rez, and included: Chinle, Dilkon, Kayenta, Shiprock, Tuba City and Window Rock.

Red Hawk Cooper was his name. He stood six foot four and weighed in at 235 pounds. An unruly tuft of black hair peeked from beneath his hat. He had a strong chin, grooves in his brow and sunken cheeks.

At fifty-five his ears and nose should have resembled an elephant's as they continue to grow forever. Only the eyes remain the same size from birth. His head had remained geometric, however.

Han Po and Jack were enjoying their third cup of coffee. Han Po seemed to be leery of the atmosphere. He mentioned that he's been ignored once before in the café and didn't wish to return. The same ones who took advantage of his hospitality in the cantina.

"Fornicate all those white-trash unappreciative freeloaders who darken my door," Han Po suddenly expounded.

Jack nodded in agreement and mentioned that everyone's the

same color when they've had enough booze in their gut. It's a great equalizer.

Juanita came by with a coffee pot and topped them off.

"That Cooper is one strange person," she said. "He comes in here every once in awhile. Orders the biggest steak. Sort of a conundrum there. Claim's he's an environmentalist and vegetarian and abhors killing animals, but look at him dig into that steak."

"You've got to figure there's a whole lot of body there to feed," Jack said. "I don't think it would be wise to tangle with him."

The plates were cleared from Cooper's table and he sat there picking his teeth. Jack wandered over to him and asked if he was intruding.

"Nope. Don't believe I've seen you around before."

"Name's Jack Collins. Do you have a card with your telephone number on it? I might have to call you some time."

"Sure do. Compliments of the rez print shop."

"What brings you into town," Jack asked. "Not that it's any of my business."

"Just so happens I've been up to the mine. Some old codger went and got himself dead. Guess he's been camping out in one of the shacks and got aholt of hantavirus. Mighty bad stuff, that."

"I never heard of that. What is it?" Jack asked, very curious.

"Well, it's mostly caused by the deer mouse. They leak and crap all over the place and pass it to humans who breathe in dust. He musta been sweeping up the place and took too much dust into his lungs. Helluva way to go, if you ask me."

"Sounds that way to me, too," Jack said with a grimace. "Anyhow, thanks for the info and the card."

"No problem. I'll be seein' ya around most likely."

CHAPTER SEVENTEEN

Ernie Conrad, his faithful Dalmatian seated alongside, pulled into the passenger pick-up area of Albuquerque International Airport. He had been dispatched by Cliff to greet and transport two guests from Louisiana.

They weren't too difficult to spot. As they emerged from the terminal they squinted through the blazing rays of sun as though they hadn't seen it for months.

"Howdy, folks. You'd be the Fountains, I opine."

"That's us alright," Harry answered, "but it's La Fontaine, you see."

"Right. Name's Ernie," he said and poked a thumb at his chest. "Well, let's get your luggage into the rig and we'll be off."

Celeste slithered into the back seat. Harry joined Ernie up front and immediately removed his tie. It was close to choking him.

"That's sure a nice dog you have there Ernie. What kind is it?" Celeste asked.

"He be a Dalmatian. They called them coach dogs in the old days. You might have seen them riding fire trucks."

"You know, even though the sun's out, it's still a bit chilly. When does it warm up around here?" Harry wanted to know.

"Bout nine or so. Then You'll wish we had air conditioning in this here rig. Cliff tole me to use the jeep, but this here Land Rover's a bit more comfy on the backside. My dog likes it better too."

They were outside the city limits now.

"Look at those magnificent animals over there, Celeste. I've never seen anything so beautiful," Harry gushed.

"Them's pronghorns," Ernie offered. Some folks call 'em antelopes, like in the song, you know. You're lucky to eyeball 'em. Ain't many herds left around here nowadays. See that one out front? He's wiggllin his white butt to warn the others there might be danger. They get to runnin' and they're fasterin hell. Sorry ma'am."

"Not that I haven't heard worse than that," she grinned.

They turned off the main highway and were now racing along an unmarked road. The endless sky was cloudless. The sun was now beating down on the vehicle like an over-zealous heat lamp.

Celeste began chuckling quietly.

"What's so funny, dear?"

"Didn't you see that sign? Some practical joker must have stuck it there."

"Guess I missed it. What was it?"

"An old Burma Shave sign. Planted way out here by itself."

Ernie grinned at her in the rearview mirror. "You'll sure enough see some strange things around here, ma'am."

Everything seemed enormous, boundless, and in all that vastness the only movement was the landscape swishing by them.

Bareness prevailed throughout the open plain, stripped clean by the prevailing northwest winds, with the exception of an occasional sage brush or mesquite.

The road snaked around several small limestone-streaked mesas. There were several areas carpeted with glittering shells as on a beach. It was learned later that these were salt water snail shells and that water, lots of it, once covered this whole area.

*   *   *

"Here we be, folks. Mr. Collins said he'd be in the café. I'll take your gear over to the motel. Be seein' ya around."

"Merci, Ernie. It's been a most interesting ride," Harry said, tongue in cheek.

They entered the café and were immediately captured in a bear hug by Jack. "Saw the Rover pull up and knew it had to be you two!"

"Mon ami, what place is this? So strange and remote. I felt like Wrong-Way Corrigan flying across the Kalahari. Everything is so far apart out here. I surmise the universe must be like this—there is no edge and there is no center. Mon dieu!"

"Come off it, Harry, it's not all that bad. You'll like it once you get used to it."

"Ignore him, Jack," Celeste urged. "He's been on edge ever since he found out they don't serve meals on the planes any more. All will be right with him after we fill his gut. You'll see."

"Geez, I hope so. And he hasn't even seen the suite I reserved in the motel," he said, twitching his nose. "Do we have to baby sit him, or will he just pout for a day or so?"

"You two can go ahead and have your laughs. They say, who laughs last—."

Juanita greeted Jack's guests with open arms. "Welcome to my humble place. I hope your stay will be most pleasant. Is it something you wish to eat?"

"Just some coffee to start, Juanita," Jack answered. "They haven't got their feet on the ground yet."

"Coffee, yes," Harry said. "And I'd like a glass of orange juice. He raised an eyebrow at Celeste. "And you also, dear?"

"Oh, yes! That sounds good."

"I didn't want to seem rude, guys, but I forgot to introduce my friend here, Mr. Han Po, who owns the cantina."

"So nice to meet you. If Jack likes you, you can't be all bad," she winked.

"I'll second that," Harry agreed.

Off to one side, Eva sat alone, engrossed as usual in writing on a legal pad. Her ballpoint pen was flitting across the page as though it had a mind of it's own. She was composing notes on her latest trek through town before they departed her memory.

Han Po placed a hand on Jack's arm and nodded in her direction. "That one is no good. *Dao ting tú shuó,* he spat out. What is heard on the road is reported to others."

Han Po has a saying in Chinese for everything," Jack explained. "You'll get to know him better, but for now, take everything he says as gospel."

Eva was in her element. Selfish and greedy. She wrote of people involved in clandestine doings—the shame of it! She felt superior to most of the women in town. She used their fears and the secrets inside their hearts.

Juanita , refilling their cups, overheard Han Po, and added, "That one is certainly a kumquat!" This was her favorite sobriquet for those she considered anti-social and uncouth. The descriptions of Eva put forth by Han Po and Juanita caused Celeste to hide her mouth behind a napkin to keep from laughing outright.

Jack caught Juanita's eye and indicated with a wave across the table that Harry and Celeste would now be ready for lunch.

She hustled to the kitchen and began assisting Dinah with the preparations.

Soon a serving table was set alongside, loaded with delicacies, most of which the two Louisianan's weren't privy to. The aromas had Celeste close to swooning.

The meal began with chili con carne and a *sopaipilla*—a pillow-shaped flour pastry that had been deep-fried and awaited a honey condiment.

For the second dish they were treated to a pork tamale—covered with green chili—with cornmeal added, then wrapped in a corn husk.

Dinah served the final dish with a flourish: an immense taco with lettuce, tomatoes, refried beans, guacamole, sour cream and green chili on a puffy tortilla.

Harry burped loudly, excused himself, and patted his stomach. "One marvelous meal, mon amie," he mentioned to Juanita. "I'm afraid, though, that I'll suffer from all the spices, although similar to Cajun cooking."

"Not to worry. Once you have eaten the chilis the natural painkilling chemical endorphin is released and your stomach will rejoice," she explained, smiling broadly. "You will soon become used to our way of cooking, I'm certain. 'Many foods should be eaten slowly to savor the flavor,' is a famous saying around here. Never get in too big a hurry to leave the table."

"What I really enjoyed was the fresh vegetables. They were just great!" Celeste mentioned.

"You must see my garden, and see where they grow," Dinah said proudly.

"Oh, yes! I'd like that."

"Follow me and I'll give you a tour."

They stepped through the kitchen and out the back door. Dinah's garden was amazing, to say the least. She explained that all her produce were genuine old-fashioned vegetables, fertilized with good old horse shit with some hybrid mule patties thrown in for good measure. She also added coffee grounds and egg shells to the mixture. Almost anything would grow on her plot.

She claimed her small patch of earth was so rich she could plant and harvest two crops a day—with time left over for a whirl at the one-armed bandit out front.

Possibly a slight exaggeration.

The cornucopia growing in her garden included bell, jalapeño, habanero and Anaheim peppers. What she considered her *pepper mates* were string beans, carrots, cauliflower, corn, garlic, lettuce, onions, squash and two varieties of tomatoes.

These vegetables got along nicely with her peppers.

This place is remarkable," Celeste said with an almost reverenced awe. "It's like an oasis here in the middle of such desolation."

"I agree," Dinah answered, nodding toward a field pump. "We used to have to urge our irrigation water out of those things, but now there's more than enough water. You see, the Estancia was built over an immense aquifer that's now providing water through the town's underground water system and kept flowing by artesian pressure."

"That's great! To think that those Spaniards, so many years ago, could figure out they were on top of all that water."

"Oh, I guess some of the things they did back then made sense, but they were cruel to the Indians and forced them to do all kinds of menial things. Now, if you don't mind, I've got to get back inside and sit for awhile. This extra baggage I'm carrying keeps me forever tired."

"Sorry. I wasn't thinking. I didn't mean to keep you so long. Here, let me get the door for you."

*   *   *

Once Jack had Harry and Celeste settled in their room, he made plans to return to the barn after dark. He pulled a mini-mag flashlight and a dark jacket out of his duffle bag.

Several hours later, when the majority of the town were in their houses asleep, he eased quietly down the street to the barn. A slight breeze winnowed some dust ahead of him. He was now familiar with the layout of the buildings and wouldn't need the flashlight just yet.

The only lights on the street were blanketed from the café and cantina.

He approached the door to the room next to his with caution, not certain if anyone was within.

It wasn't a simple me or them barrier.

The latch was unlocked. Very strange. Perhaps they figured no one would be so bold as to enter uninvited.

Nothing wraps a man in such a mist of errors as his own curiosity in searching for things beyond him.

To hell with it! I've come this far.

He pulled the door open. It rasped loudly on worn hinges. Then a strange sound as of a whirlwind. There were bats! Hundreds of them! He ducked to avoid the onrush. He laid spread-eagled just inside the door; his face pressed into evapotranspiration straw and dirt.

Silhouettes against the waning moon filled the sky, dipping here and there, searching for bugs, mosquitoes, gnats. Anything to appease their appetites.

When he finally rose up, he was smothered in dust—his face the appearance of a mime—only his eyes visible.

He inched toward the rear of the room, following the thin beam of light from his flashlight. In the vicinity where he had observed the three men at work, he tapped on the boards until he heard a dull thud. He determined they hadn't nailed the board back. He eased his fingers along the edge and pulled it loose. Inside the depression were about a dozen parcels wrapped in heavy plastic. Best I don't disturb them. I'll wait until I've got help or some law to back me up.

Placing the board back, he eased out of the room and closed the door. He was now sweating profusely and the dust on his face was turning to mud.

He retraced his steps back to the motel and took a long, hot shower.

CHAPTER EIGHTEEN

Jack came up to Juanita, a look of concern on his face.

"Where's Dinah? She's not in the kitchen. She hasn't had the kid already, has she?"

"No. She still has time. She felt a little weak so I gave her the day off. You act like you're her sugar daddy, Jack."

"I wouldn't say that," he answered, slightly offended, but with a hearty laugh. "I just want to make sure she's around tomorrow."

"Why's that?"

"I'm setting up a wedding between her and that soldier she sort of got involved with. He'll be here tomorrow along with the base chaplain. I figured a nice, quiet affair would suit them just fine."

Ears tuned in from across the room. Eva was busy collating notes from last night and overheard the conversation. She caressed the word *wedding*. It would be all over town. She would be in her glory!

"Could you tell me where she lives? I'll wander over there and break the news so she doesn't get too much of a shock."

"You mean to tell me she doesn't even have a clue of what you're up to?"

Juanita was aghast.

"Probably not. I sort of hinted to her last week, but didn't get a rise."

"You're something else, Jack! Mister Goodfella. Have you thought about any kind of reception—that is, if they both agree to your scheme?"

"Yup. Han Po is going to set something up. Said he's even going to have the floor swept. Maybe you can get together with him and figure out some snacks?"

"Bet your sweet ass! There's no way my crew is going to miss out on such a big celebration."

"Good show. We'll give those young lovers a real blast, huh?"

*   *   *

"Mind if I come in for a minute?"

"Hi there, Jack. Of course not, come right in. I'm not really ready for visitors, but make yourself at home. I'll put on some coffee."

"Don't bother. I'm full up. Just came from the café. Sit. Please. I've got something important to say to you."

"You're sure mysterious today. What's got you so up tight?"

In his rather brusque manner he explained that he'd contacted the soldier from Fort Huachuca and that he was agreeable to his plan of a wedding.

"I'm trying to be as diplomatic as possible, but I'm afraid I get low marks for that," he scowled.

She tilted her head and regarded him through narrowed eyes. "Well, I declare! You sure have taken matters into your own hands. Did you ever think that one or both of us would shoot your plan down?"

"Sure. Gave it some thought—about thirty-seconds worth—but who'd turn down an offer like this? If you two can't seem to get along, at least the kid will have a name—and parents. You've got to realize, too, that every mother is a woman. I figured that out all by myself."

She grimaced, but didn't reply.

He produced a faint smile and headed out. She saw him off at the door and closed it firmly; breathed a sigh, happy to be alone with her thoughts.

After Jack left her house, Dinah was caught between two images.

If she went through with the ceremony at least the child within her would be legal.

Early on in the pregnancy she'd contacted an old widow of a Welshman, killed at the mine, who told her she would perform an abortion for a few dollars. It wouldn't be the best of decisions then, and besides, it was way past time for that now.

And there was always the concern of scandal to consider. She caught sight of herself in the small mirror near the bathroom door and thought perhaps, Mr. Collins was probably doing the best thing for all concerned. Notwithstanding his meddling.

Whatever his reasons she smiled at her image. She hadn't smiled like that for a long time; since discovering the change taking place in her body. She was still half-smiling long after he was gone.

The smile lingered on her lips as she climbed into bed. The miracle of two people living within her body was sufficient to leave her content.

*   *   *

Corporal Anderson and the Chaplain were making good time on the route from Sierra Vista, so Pete decided to swing into Gallup. He bought a handmade lace shawl for Dinah as a reverse dowry—knowing full well she wouldn't have access to anything close to wedding apparel at the mercantile.

He still had second thoughts about Mr. Collins' arrangements. While still in puberty, his mother told him that love doesn't just happen. You have to grow into it.

*   *   *

Celeste arose around eight o'clock. Unusually late for her. She stepped out of the room and was blasted instantly by the sun as it slammed her face and scalp like a hammer.

A hat would be necessary.

She heard the fullness of silence as she wandered into town. The buildings of the Estancia and town were equally divided between stucco and adobe with *Azoteas*—red-tiled pentile roofs—and small houses with clapboard siding, remnants of the time when the mine was operational.

Shadows crept up the yellow stucco walls. There were large areas where it had cracked and pulled away.

Small cumulus clouds decorated the sky.

Eventually her wanderings brought her back to the main street and the café. A curlicue of smoke rose gently from the chimney. A woman sitting alone indicated the empty chair at her table and Celeste acquiesced to the offer.

"Hello there. I'm Naomi. I assume you're the one visiting Jack?"

"Yes, as a matter of fact. My name's Celeste. He and my husband are still asleep, so I thought I'd wander around a bit and check things out."

"That's good. Always nice to know the layout of the land, eh?"

"Not that so much. I just wasn't quite ready for breakfast."

Naomi struck her as entirely feminine. She had an extraordinary androgynous body with the muscle tone of an Olympian hidden beneath her clothes, however, she was all woman to the casual observer—not just feminine.

"You'll most likely hear things about me before long, so I might as well set the record straight right off. I run the cat house west of town. What? No raised eyebrows?"

"I don't judge people by what they do, but what they are," Celeste answered. "Some of my best friends back home are in shady occupations, but I don't hold that against them."

"You know, I think we'll get along just fine, Celeste. Anyhow, out here in the desert we're all equal. I figure the only unnatural sexual behavior is none at all." She laughed loudly at her own observation.

Although a handsome woman in her own right, she was no match to Celeste's beauty. They were getting along famously regardless of their being moral opposites and their attitude towards sex.

Ole Oleson was perched at his usual table near the front window. A ragged, skinny man entered the café and stood scanning the interior. He had a pockmarked face, the result of a childhood etching from smallpox. Juanita approached him and asked what he wanted.

"Nothing yet, sweets. I'll just see if that huge gentleman by the window will spring for a cuppa coffee."

"I wouldn't—," she started to say.

Without so much as a howdy-do, he went over to Ole and asked him politely if he'd buy him a cup of coffee.

"No way, bum! I don't give alms to your type."

"How so? Looks like you can afford it."

"Mebbee so. I'll tell you what, shrimp. If you're willing to put in a few hours work, I just might treat you to a breakfast."

"Done."

He started for the empty chair.

"Not here. Sit over there. I can't stand the stench of you. After you eat, I'd suggest you get close to some soap and water before I haul you out to the ranch. By the way, what do they call you?"

"Name's Frenchy Burgoyne."

"Good enough. I'm Mr. Oleson to you."

"Well, Mr. Oleson, you won't regret it. I'm a good worker."

"Better be or I'll feed you to the hogs."

Chapter Nineteen

The rental car pulled up just as Harry was entering the café, exuding the aroma of his après-resar, hair slicked back with pomade, after his recent shower.

Celeste was deep into a platter of biscuits and gravy.

"That surely looks good. Think I'll have the same. What's with the two soldiers who just pulled up outside?"

"According to the woman I was just talking to, it's the start of a wedding. The cook and that Corporal are about to tie the knot."

"Well now, seems we got into town just in time. I don't suppose Jack's got anything to do with it, do you? He's being extra cautious with his shaving and even laid out some clean duds."

"Oh, but of course he does. He's the one who set it up. You know how he is—."

Jack introduced himself to the Chaplain, Major Lipscomb, and Corporal Anderson.

"Padre, I don't know if you'll go along with this idea of mine, but as far as I'm concerned the church is off-limits for the wedding. I'm thinking of holding it right here, if you don't mind."

"There's something wrong with the church, Mr. Collins?"

"Not so much the church as it is with the so-called priest. He's a phony as far as I'm concerned. Gives the place a bad name. Anyhow, I was told that the Corporal here is a Protestant."

While they were talking at the door, Juanita had a few customers help arrange the tables and chairs in a more suitable attitude. Her place and the cantina were doing a brisk business in anticipation of the nuptials. Nothing this grand had taken place around here for—it seemed ages.

"I don't have any objections, at all. The place of the ceremony is of little importance. As long as it's observed with decorum and by an appointed man of the cloth. I say, let's get on with it!"

Of course, the whole town was invited. The few men who had suits, wore them, along with freshly ironed shirts. Those without suits were in clean jeans and their best faded shirts.

The women were clad in their Sunday dresses—or Monday mundane's, as the case may be. Children whirled among the tables and adults like dervishes, anxious for the ceremony to end so they could check out the food being prepared next door.

Timco was in town and was tending the spits behind the cantina. Two plump pigs were in a roasting attitude. There were some comments later about the huge gap in the top of one pig. It seems Tinco had sliced off several pork chops and a goodly portion of fat back—for frying up cracklins—to present to the workers at the site who couldn't make it to the event personally.

A wild turkey and several sage hens were roasting on a grill inside half of a 55-gallon drum propped up on pipe legs. Someone had donated a hind quarter from a cull milk cow to become part of the feast.

Timco soon had a covey of chirping, gossiping cooks helping with the chores. Extra mesquite fires were blazing. Hung over flames were large cast-iron pots filled with all kinds of delicious food.

Somewhat overly obese, Alice One Wing Butterfly was flitting among all the cooks advising them of spices and doneness of their offerings. She wasn't about to be ignored in her self-appointed duties.

Main street was clogged with vehicles of all shapes and sizes; cars, wagons and pickups were pulled in haphazardly, blocking the street as drivers, part of the busy, noisy throng were seeking ingress to the café. Horses were hitched to anything static.

It seems word got out by tom-tom and smoke signal. Half the Navajo Nation and a large portion of border Mexicans, along with gaunt ranchers and their coveys of kids and pets—which Midnight ignored—were jostling for position, all hell-bent to attend the wedding and partake of the victuals.

A slight exaggeration, perhaps.

The actual count probably came closer to sixty-five.

The ceremony was proceeding. Corporal Anderson was enjoying his own wedding almost as much as a corpse enjoys a wake. He was overwhelmed with so many people milling about, shaking his hand and kissing Dinah. It was to be a simple affair and it had turned into a carnival, of sorts.

Dinah was so happy she didn't notice anyone else except Peter, standing erect at her side.

There were I do's and rice tossed. The susurrus was replaced with hullabaloo.

The mob adjourned to the cantina where Han Po had set up plank tables, on top of beer cases, covered with sheets.

Music was provided by the same group that had accompanied Wei, with the addition of a fiddle player. The banjo player's left hand rested on the fretboard, while his right, grasping a plectrum, was strumming up a storm.

Dinah managed to break away and sneaked out back.

"Timco, I'm really nervous. It just doesn't feel right. Me on my wedding day, and sticking out like a blimp!" she whimpered. "Do you think everything will work out?"

"Not to worry, little one. Everyone knows that when you become a housewife you automatically put on a pound or two and formally lose a tooth for each baby born. It is written."

She smiled. "You're such a wise and nice person. Thanks for just taking a bit of time with me. I feel better already. Best I get back inside to my new husband."

She hugged him fiercely.

"That would probably be a good idea, before they send out a posse."

The men, and a few women, were drinking beer. Some had shooters of whiskey or tequila raised in salute to the bride and groom. A large bowl of punch was available for the non-drinkers. Unbeknownst to the teetotalers, it had been spiked generously.

The young busboy from the café sipped ginger ale, nodding at people as they wandered by, not expecting a response. He wiped an imaginary spot off his clean jeans. This was his first wedding reception and he was enjoying it to the fullest.

When the food began to arrive, someone mentioned that one of the pigs looked a whole lot like Susie, the town's resident mascot, who had the run of the place. Seems nobody would claim to have butchered her since they'd be hung out to dry in the square the next day; a feast for the blue flies. Cliff sidled up to a weaving Jack, his usual saturnine countenance of gloom and morose enveloping his head. His speech was thinned to a gossamer membrane.

"You're on the sauce."

"So are you, sheeny. We Catholics like to get snockered every once in awhile to give the priest something to preach about Sunday."

Han Po was enjoying the libations. More so the constant ringing of the cash register. "Nice people, Jack."

"Yeh. Almost as nice as their horses, I guess," he slurred.

Overhead a chevron of geese were heading northwest, in lieu of a jet flyover, to celebrate proceedings. Out in the street, a man caught up in the revelry, grabs his carbine from the saddle holster and brings down a weather cock atop the roof of a building with a single shot. It meets the street with a terrific crash. The scene in front of the cantina immediately freezes.

Someone yells from the crowd, "No harm, no foul! Let's get back inside to the booze!"

The band was playing a waltz for the newlyweds but Pete didn't know how and tried a slow Texas two-step, afraid to jostle Dinah too harshly.

Major Lipscomb eased the couple aside. "After all this commotion, I'm sure you two could stand a bit of peace and quiet. I suggest we get over to Dinah's place and load up a few personal items and head down to the fort. She's a legal dependent now, and is entitled to prime services at the hospital."

"Where's the bride and groom?"

"I seen them and the Chaplain headin' outta town."

"Luna de miel. Si. They will honeymoon in the car, yes?"

Chapter Twenty

It was two days after the big event. The town, as a whole, settled back into it's normal boring routine.

Harry and Celeste seemed to be enjoying the solitude of the unique area.

Cliff, out of the kindness of his heart, offered them a jeep—at a reasonable rate, of course. "You folks should get out and about. Enjoy some of this fine country."

"We'll do just that, Mr. Workman. Jack tells me there's a bit of fishing in the nearby river, and we might take a run over there."

"Certainly. Be cautious though. There might be a snake or two sunning on the sand."

"We'll be very careful, thank you."

They sat there for awhile sipping coffee. Cliff was entertaining erotic thoughts about Celeste. Seeing her, one would immediately think of a bedroom, for which she was ideally suited. She appeared to him as a free-spirited nymph. He wondered if she would go skinny-dipping in the river. That would be a sight to behold!

"You seem to be involved in almost everything around here, Cliff. Just what's your interest?" Harry asked him.

"Well, there's them that want—and then, there's them that got. I got!" he answered emphatically. "There's also them in hell that want ice water. I don't supply that. Too costly to transport. I try to keep my eyes peeled for opportunities. I run a small operation, actually. Got a few pieces of equipment, some vehicles and lots of contacts.

"Besides a contract with the Post Office to run two rural service routes, I manage to keep the small ranches supplied with propane, diesel, gas and sometimes have my drivers run supply jaunts into Albuquerque for a small fee.

He leaned back in his chair, a look of complete satisfaction on his face.

Harry and Celeste shared an uneasy burst of laughter. Not so much from enjoying Cliff's entrepreneur-like statements as from his jumpy manner. His eyes and hands were in constant motion.

Juanita refilled their cups.

"Who's the new gal in the kitchen?" Cliff asked her.

"That'd be Mindy. She's Dinah's replacement. Dinah never did like taking the time to make up menudo, so Mandy took on the chore. Now she's here full time. We serve lots of it on Sunday morning. Excellent for hangovers, and some even claim it's the breakfast of champions."

"I don't know about that breakfast for champions bit, I can scarf it anytime," Cliff beamed.

Of course, Eva had things to write about Mindy. Probably out of defense against her own self-imposed loneliness. She recorded that Mindy was a very loose woman, full of lust and forever cohabitating.

*   *   *

Doc called two of his extensive contacts at State and made arrangements with them to utilize some of the idle equipment parked near Naomi's compound.

He explained there was a qualified operator on site who had worked at the uranium mine. Approval was granted.

Cliff was asked to bring around a new battery, some oil, and a can of clean fuel for the grader the next time he came out Estancia way.

During a conversation with Juanita, Doc was told that Mike

Plunkett, a former mine worker, was available. When Doc approached Mike in the cantina, he was a bit surprised to find him sipping coke.

It seems Mike spent some time in the loony bin.

"Sure," he admitted." They put me away for awhile, claiming I was psychotic, but I snookered them alright. I was just a born-again dipso and couldn't stay off the sauce. There wasn't nothing wrong with my head. It was my gut that needed attention."

Mike was a unique specimen of humanity. He always wore shades. Large ones that wrapped around his face. He had a benign, dime-sized mole in the center of his forehead giving him the appearance of a Cyclops with his eyes covered the way they were. He had an immense, fleshy proboscis and narrow, severe lips.

When the battery, fuel and oil arrived, Doc went with Mike to the grader and parked his butt on a skip loader while preparations were taking place. With the battery installed, the dip stick eye-balled and five gallons of fresh fuel in the tank, it was time to check things out.

Mike sat on the seat, smoking a cheroot casually, and counted to himself. When he figured the time was right, he pushed the glo-plug switch and waited. Then he hit the starter button. The neglected engine growled a few times and finally kicked over.

A wheeze.

A belch of black smoke enveloped Doc who now had the look of a coal miner.

With a wide, toothy grin, Mike asked, "Whaddya think?"

"You're hired. First job will be to cut a halfway decent road out to the digs so vehicles can make it there without busting an axle. Can you handle that?"

"Damned straight! Can do, Doc. I'm right on it!"

Plunkett was a strange one, that's for sure. Hardly ever seen in the company of another. He had spooned his wife for eight years and she finally accepted. Three days after returning from their honeymoon, she was in the outhouse, when lightning struck it and fried her ass. He never got over it and avoided women with a passion from that point on.

CHAPTER TWENTY-ONE

Doc and Yellow Fox were sitting cross-legged on a four by eight piece of plywood studying a large-scale plot of the digs. The sheet of paper was anchored at the corners with small rocks. By using two fluxgate magnetometers—commonly used for archaeological prospecting—they managed to outline some of the underground structures. Small indicator flags marked the strategic areas.

They were back.

Perched behind a slight rise, out of sight.

The motley group talked quietly amongst themselves—spitting into the sand—scratching their crotches—rubbing their hands together in anticipation.

Chollo hissed for attention. "Make a little mouth. Don't talk so loud. Observe, amigos, how he peels an orange," as he motioned towards Doc. "So mucho precision, yes? Almost as though an operation by a brain surgeon is in progress."

Raif, the unwashed one, palmed a stiletto, and with the grace of a toreo preparing to thrust his estocada into the bull's aorta, moved his feet into a defensive position, but took no further steps in Doc's direction.

There would be no olé cheer.

One of the banditos bore the sunken cheeks and jaundiced eyes of an ill person. He spat large globs of phlegm into the sand, evidenced in advanced TB.

They approached cautiously.

"What are you seeking, señor? Perhaps treasure?" Chollo asked.

His head seemed to sprout directly from his shoulders without bothering itself with the trouble of a neck.

"That shouldn't be a question for you people. The question should be, 'How soon should we leave this place?' Doc countered. "You might consider a rapid departure. There is a solution to your dilemma, however."

"And that would be, señor?"

"Drop your weapons and leave peacefully."

"Ah, but that would be most foolish," he smirked at his companions.

"Not so," Doc said quietly.

From behind the group, Timco cautioned them in a threatening tone, "I'll take one and possibly two to their last cantina if you don't listen to my friend," he said, leveling a double-barrel 12-gauge at them. "Which will it be? I let you go without skinning you the last time, and now you're foolish enough to return. Choose!"

"I see you have used Apache tactics, breed," Chollo stated. He looked askance for a brief moment. "It is my honest opinion, compadres, we should obey and leave."

He twisted his mustache with his left hand and indicated the horses with his right.

The three banditos stepped into their stirrups together like well-trained, synchronized ballet dancers, turned their horse's heads, and were soon disappearing into a cloud of dust.

"I get my jollies when a scheme comes together," Timco murmured.

*   *   *

They were in the diminutive, although comfortable, motel office. Ruby was getting acquainted with Harry and Celeste. She announced she was getting fat, so her horses must need some exercise.

"Do you folks ride?"

"Oui. We are both adequate riders," Celeste answered, proud of the fact they weren't complete hicks from the east.

"That's good. I was planning on riding out to see Doc at the digs tomorrow. If you want, I'll have horses saddled for you."

"That's a splendid idea!" Celeste chirped. "I'll have to visit the mercantile to buy one hat, but otherwise I'm ready. Harry goes as is."

"Good. Then that's settled. I've got a bit of paperwork to take care of, but I'll probably see you later in the cantina."

Chapter Twenty-Two

"Saddle up the Morgans for our two guests, Alfredo."

The Morgans were magnificent horses and her pride and joy; one a chestnut, the other a bay.

"I'll habla with the beasts for them to behave nicely, yeh? I'll be taking the Cayuse for it's first trail ride. I think maybe the buckskin will do for Jack."

Alfredo was no longer a hobbledehoy. He had now worked for Ruby the better part of four years. He was tall and strong with burning dark eyes that could penetrate any negative attitude a young woman might have towards him. It was no wonder he had become the pursuer, and had discovered the pleasures of the flesh.

His great-grandparents received manumission, of which he wasn't aware, having been brought up free and easy.

The Cayuse Indian Pony was donated to Ruby by the Wild Horse Research Center in Porterville, California. Her fame working with horses had reached the Center and they approached her to try selective breeding to help protect the herd from extinction.

Today, the breed is seldom seen outside California. Only a handful are even still in existence. Ruby would find this an extremely pleasant and easy seat. The horse was a roan, heavily muscled, and although only fourteen hands high, was quite powerful.

Before they were ready to ride out, Han Po showed up at the corral and asked meekly if he could join them. It would be a welcome adventure from the mundane cantina routine, he explained.

"I overheard you talking last night and would like to join you."

"You know, Han Po, it could be a bit hazardous out on the trail, and I'm not sure I want to take responsibility for you," Ruby cautioned.

"Fornicate all hazards. If I fall onto my celestial ass, I won't hold you responsible, large woman."

After considerable deliberation, she acquiesced.

"Okay, Alfredo, put a saddle on the jenny. That should suit you, Han Po. She won't move any faster than her stomach dictates. Put a small sack of oats in the saddle bag, but don't let her see it until we're in camp or she'll put on the brakes and you won't get her moving for God knows how long."

Harry and Celeste sat quietly in their saddles waiting for the word to move out. The withers of the horses were atremble, anxious to hit the trail.

Ruby explained to them that the Morgans were her best trail horses. Gentle, surefooted and intelligent. "They won't lose you if you doze in the saddle."

While Alfredo was equipping the jenny, Jack's horse pawed the ground impatiently. The young buckskin was also eager to get going. His face was sharply chiseled, with flaring nostrils. His eyes were inky black, deep as pools, and gave no indication of familiarity towards the possible rider. Ruby told Jack to bend an ear to calm him down. He was finally allowed to climb aboard the swaying back of the spirited animal after a great show of reluctance.

At last, the parade was ready to get underway.

Han Po on the jenny would take up the rear. The animal sensed his anxiety. They cantered off as though entered in the Camptown Races. Han Po smiled broadly and began to sing: "G'wine to run all night— do dah, do dah"— hopelessly off key.

As they rode out of the corral, a chorus line of crows sat gossiping on the fence, heedless of all the excitement amongst the humans.

After clearing the confines of Ruby's fenced quarter section, the land beneath the horse's hooves appeared to be undulating. In no stretch of the imagination was it flat.

The digs were probably no more than sixteen miles from town, as the crow flies, however, detours around two small mesas and working past a few dry washes increased the mileage considerably.

Ruby was following the diminishing tracks made by Cliff's truck closely, but she cut across in a few places. Spots where the truck balked and refused to obey. The surrounding area was like a barren lunar landscape. In it's own way, beautiful. A harsh beauty. A dangerous beauty.

To the east a small dust devil churned the sky and danced across the land.

The horses kicked up the fine, dry earth into a brown cloud that clung to the trail behind them, enveloping Han Po, some one hundred yards in the rear.

Large Ruby's horses weren't the best on a trail but let them get their noses into a feed bag and they became oat-eating machines.

Very efficient.

They'd been idle too long and their memories needed to be re-schooled to rider's commands. Their skittishness settled down after awhile and they calmed to an easy trot.

Ruby was enjoying the gait of the Cayuse. She obviously had phimosis from the rhythm and hummed quietly to herself, smiling inwardly.

CHAPTER TWENTY-THREE

After crossing the languid Deception River, they entered the large canyon in which the digs were located.

Doc and Timco were surprised to see the group ride up. The seven students from the university and the Basque twins stopped work and began to saunter over.

"Get your lazy asses in gear and back to work!" Doc admonished.

"Do you have to be so hard on them, Doc? They just wanted to greet us," Ruby stated.

"I don't fraternize with the workers, per se. You have to keep on top of them or they'll screw around and get nothing accomplished."

"Sure, but a little familiarity eases the tension and they might even give you more production."

"You've got to realize, Large, that these kids are untrained, without the slightest notion of what's required of them."

"It shouldn't take them too long to figure out how to use those *technical* shovels and picks. It's mostly muscle work at this stage, isn't it" she said, with a slight grin.

"Sure, but I'd like a bit more respect. After all, I'm the one who has to take the heat if something screws up."

It was apparent the overly educated Doc was a veritable bastion of the project, although he lacked diplomacy.

Among his student workers, Ruth Golden Eagle was the only one with previous dig experience. He nominated her as foreman. She cautioned the group to go easily and carefully to avoid damaging any bones or shards they might encounter.

Timco led the animals to the limited shade of the partially completed Quonset and tethered them to a small cedar.

Han Po was cussing loudly, swatting at several mosquitoes circling his head in formation. He was reminded by Doc that the pesky things also thrive in the Arctic, and there is no escape.

"Here, slap some of this citronella on your exposed skin. It might help a bit."

"I didn't ride all the way out here to be eaten alive by these miniature man-eating buzzards," he growled.

Doc ignored the outburst.

*   *   *

Timco nominated himself as the camp cocinero. With a wink at Edur, the youngest of the twins by two minutes, he motioned him over.

He gave him a slight pinch on the arm and said, "Bruha! This is going to work out just fine. Now I've got me a messcook to keep me company. You can start on those pots and pans. I hate doing them, Makes my hands turn into prunes."

"Okay. Where's the soap at?"

"Soap! We don't got some. Use sand and some ashes from the fires. Works like a champ. When you're done with that chore, step over here and I'll show you how to make biscuits."

He had a large cast-iron pot of pinto beans, garnished with bacon and onion, hanging over one of the fires, simmering. The aroma would cause a rock to salivate.

Celeste and Ruby wandered away from the excavations and joined Timco in his kitchen area. He handed them each a tin cup of coffee and offered camp stools.

"You sure have this place fixed up homey-like," Celeste said.

"I've done my share of hobo cooking along the way, but this is like heaven. I've got everything I need right here in this chest. After I set up in the Quonset I'll be more organized and the workers will be eating like they was at the Ritz."

Edur was ready for his lesson.

"Watch closely. I'm only going to show you one time. After that, you're on your own. If you screw up, get ready to duck, 'cause the troops will start heaving stuff at your thick skull."

"Okay, Yellow Fox. I'll pay attention," Erdu said, scratching his head. There sure was a lot to learn about camp cooking [he thought].

The self-appointed cocinero tossed a handful of flour on the table and then set the Dutch oven on the fire to heat. In the meantime he made a batch of dough and flattened it out. With a tin cup he cut biscuit shapes and set them aside.

When the oven was hot enough, he set the biscuits into the bottom and watched to make sure they were browning properly, and then flipped them over. When all was ready he set the tight-fitting lid on and then put some coals on top.

In about ten minutes he removed the oven from the fire, careful not to burn his hands, and lifted the lid using a piece of burlap. The biscuits were removed and set on a tin plate.

"You ladies want to sample the results? I can guarantee you'll think they're lip-smackin' good."

They were careful as the biscuits were still quite hot.

"Here," he said, handing Ruby a container and a spoon. "Top it off with some of this honey."

After a bit of lunch, Harry and Jack went back to digging. A portion of the north wall was already uncovered to a depth of five or six feet.

Although Harry was out of his element, he was enjoying the physical work thoroughly. He needed to get something on his exposed skin. It was turning bright crimson. His long-sleeved shirt helped some, but his forehead and neck were going to invade his sleep. They had the appearance of a red pepper from Dinah's garden.

After an hour, Jack took Harry aside. "I've been doing a bit of snooping and I'm not exactly happy about having that priest on the loose. He's up to something shady and in cahoots with Renaldo, the mechanic. When you get back to town, how's about checking around and see what you can find out, okay?"

"Oui. I suppose I can sort of nose around if you think it's necessary."

"You might come up with something really interesting."

*   *   *

Harry and Celeste convoyed Han Po back to town. They rode slowly through some chapparal. In places there were cats claw acacias along with the aroma of other desert flora: piñon resin, cliffrose and claret cup cactus. The air was fragrant with mesquite and the aromatic odor of cedar.

Half way to town they were strafed by a brisk breeze that produced flying sand and other bits of debris, causing them to squint and cover their mouths.

The sun was setting, changing the sky's colors moment by moment, in a phantasmagoria of hues starting with shell pink, darkening to rose red, and deepening into a rich purple, before the final light faded and the first evening stars peeked out.

After handing the animals over to Alfredo, the three weary travelers made a swift retreat to the cantina and ordered up beers. Their throats were scratchy and dry and eyes were swollen and full of grit.

Harry placed his cool bottle against his brow, temporarily relieving the scorched skin. Estelle brought Han Po his required Mason jar. Celeste ran a paper napkin around her sweaty bottle and used the wet instrument to wipe some of the grit from her face.

She peered through her half-closed eyes, and said, to Han Po, "I notice everyone uses both your names when they talk to you. What do you really like to be called?"

"Well, young lady, in China the name of the family always precedes the given name. Therefore, I'd prefer to be called Po, the glorious name given to me at birth."

"That's easy enough to remember. From now on, it's Po without the Han to confuse me," she grinned.

"Agreed! That's just between the two of us though, yeh?"

"Enough chatter, let's order up another of these delicious beers, just to whet our appetites, before we clean up. I'm ready for a meal!"

CHAPTER TWENTY-FOUR

Harry met with Renaldo. There were two strangers lazing in the room. "They work for you?" he asked..

"Nah. Haven't seen 'em before. They came in for some help on a dead truck."

"Then you don't know them?"

"I don't have the foggiest. All white men look alike to me."

"Right. You seem to keep busy. Is there that much mechanical work to be done around here?"

Renaldo took time to spit a torrent, missing Harry's shoes by a mere fraction of an inch.

"Not so many. I sorta keep busy with animals, mostly." His language was in agony as though he feared talking.

"I was just a bit curious. Probably a bit nosy too. I'll be moving on now. See you around town."

He walked off in the direction of the church . It was sweltering and he was drowning in sweat.

He appeared in the doorway of the schoolroom, blocking the slanting rectangle of mid-day light.

There were eleven students. The ersatz priest, wearing a white suplice over a black cassock, was attempting to instill the youngsters with a bit of history, and having a terrible time of it. He was overly excited.

His myopia didn't take into consideration that the two older students knew their lessons much better than he did. He was unfazed.

Harry motioned him to the back of the room.

"When you're done here, I'd like a word with you. Perhaps in your quarters?"

"I guess that wouldn't be too hard on me. I've got a slow day from now on."

They met a half hour later. The so-called priest was now wearing another outfit. Over his alb he wore a chasuble—sleeveless—of maroon, a lappet around his neck. He held a crosier of ebony inlaid with small pieces of turquoise. All items belonging to the previous priest, no doubt.

It appeared he was going through the entire wardrobe in an effort to seem holy, and by no stretch of the imagination were they his. Never one to miss out on trivial details, Harry noticed one of his fingers had a tattoo on the knuckle, an indication he had been incarcerated in the caboose at one time.

There was the beginning of a tic at his left eye.

Jack gave Harry as many details of the situation as he'd managed so far, along with the telephone number of the policeman, Red Hawke Cooper.

"Officer Cooper, my name is Harry LaFontaine. I'm a retired detective from Baton Rouge. I'm visiting a friend of mine, Jack Collins, who you met.

"The reason I'm calling is, Jack has run into a situation that he thinks needs looking in to. There seems to be drugs involved. The gist of the matter is, there's a connection between the mechanic, Dominquez, and the man who claims to be the priest.

"I'm alerting you to the fact I'll be looking into this mess, unofficially of course, and wanted to keep you apprised. I'll be rattling some cages."

"That's fine by me, Mr. LaFontaine. Just be sure you proceed with caution. I'll be available for backup if you need it. Call me anytime. Are you carrying?"

"No. But I'll take it easy. Thanks."

He opened the conversation with the priest without preamble.

"How long have you been at this parish, if I may ask?"

"What is it to you? You're sure one nosy son-of-a bitch, you know."

"My, such language from a man of the cloth. I believe you're a full-blown heretic. You slander God with your cursing, while wearing the clothes of the church, which I'm sure don't belong to you."

"What the hell do you know!"

Harry watched the man's face change. Anger, mischief, fear, guilt: triumph. He might as well rile him completely.

"I have the feeling you have preference for sexual congress with goats, or perhaps, you're a necrophiliac. I also noticed the young boys stayed way from you in school. I think you're one repulsive person."

There was a supercilious reaction to Harry's statement.

Making an effort to rein in his anger, the priest replied, "In the church, very often, devotion replaces intelligence, as I'm sure you're aware of."

The arcane of this statement brought a smile to Harry's face.

"Where did you read that? In some comic book?"

While the priest was being confronted his foot tapped like a metronome. A foot encased in a brown wing-tip shoe, no less!

"I don't know who in hell you are, mister, but I'd suggest you leave before I get real pissed and have to toss your ass out!"

"Violence is capable of consuming everyone—don't you agree?"

"Not me, friend. I'm usually calm."

When he got curious, his sentences shrank. Harry was certainly getting to him.

"Very well. I see we aren't agreeing on anything. Most certainly you'll see me around again."

*   *   *

While Harry was snooping, Celeste sat in the café chatting with Naomi. She found her interesting.

"I'm getting impatient with that man, Han Po."

"Why's that?"

"I'm down to three girls at the crib and can't seem to keep my customers happy. Them cowboys like a little choice now and then. Sorta like picking out a good cutting horse. I offered to take a couple waitresses off the Chinaman's hands, but he refuses. Says they're part of his family. Bull shit!"

"Aren't there any other girls you can put to work? It seems I saw a few unattached ones at the wedding."

"Don't like recruiting from the locals. Causes bad feelings. I'll make a run into Gallup or Albuquerque one of these days and see what comes up."

"Oh, you'll manage somehow. You seem to have a mind for business."

"Speaking of business, there's word going around about Juanita. Seems she's the total owner of all the land around here for miles."

Celeste raised a questioning eyebrow. "She must be worth millions, if that's true. Why does she run this place?"

"Just to keep her hand in, I reckon. The whole area comes under a Land Grant given to one of her distant relatives, about 400 years ago, and she's the only survivor."

"How does that work? The land grant, I mean."

"Well, throughout history governments have given land to certain citizens as a reward for service. The way I understand it, when Spain re-conquered New Mexico in 1692, the powers that be gave out several grants. Juanita's relative passed the requirement that you had to physically step on the land and make a vow to work it."

"That must have been quite a deal back then. Sort of like the Homestead Act, I guess."

"You got that right."

"Thanks for the history lesson. You must learn many choice things in your line of work. Some of those customers must be more than just cowboys, I'll wager."

"Oh, I manage to get by without advertising. It's an old and not too honorable profession, but it pays well."

She grinned, displaying a gold incisor.

Chapter Twenty-Five

Fire!

June Dombrosky, one of the older girls, noticed smoke coming from the front of the room; from beneath the door to the vestibule.

"Follow me!" she yelled, and tucked one of the younger kids under an arm.

Now there was smoke billowing from around the door that connected to the nave. The priest probably dropped a half-finished cigarette onto a stack of papers in the vestibule and it had combusted. He was always sneaking off for a quick smoke.

Rushing to the front of the room, June called for help to move the cumbersome desk covering a trap door. She had been told of this trap door by her father while he related some of the town's history.

Gasping for air, they managed to shove the desk out of the way.

She grabbed the State flag from it's stand and wrapped it around the staff. Then she told the kids to climb down the ladder into the tunnel below.

In a few quick steps she neared the door, flung it open, and lit her jury-rigged torch. When all the kids were safely below, she led them to safety, cautioning them to stay close.

The tunnel had been dug by the Indians back in the 1600's to avoid slaughter by the Spanish, who were raping the countryside.

There were small Gothic-like niches along the walls that had once, presumably, held icons. Above the niches the walls were blackened from candle smoke. The tunnel was short—maybe seventy-five feet long—and came up under a crypt in the dilapidated cemetery.

As the children popped up into the crypt and out into bright sunlight, an oldish man, tending one of the graves, asked, "Where are all you kids coming from? You scared me half to death."

"We came through the tunnel from the school," one of them answered. "There's a fire there," and she wept with fear.

"My God! Hurry and go to the café. You'll be safe there."

Panting in his haste, the corpulent man, hat askew, chest hurting, legs about to give out in panic, told himself to slow down before he had a heart attack. He scuttled on, eventually to reach the door of the café.

He stopped briefly to wipe his brow.

When he entered, the air was heavy with the smells of cooking fat, spices and simmering pots of meat and entrails, the makings of menudo.

The new cook was busy.

His shirt was matted in sweat, his face florid. The sole of one shoe had become displaced. As he shuffled it flapped in the air like the bill of a platypus.

From the rear of the room someone muttered, "I've never seen Henry waddle so fast before. The old fart must have seen a ghost or his lady threw him out—again."

A ripple—a burst of chuckles from those present.

"Help!" he finally managed to gasp. "There's a fire in the school! I sent the kids here so they would be safe."

"Where was that numb-nutted priest?"

"Didn't see him around anywheres. Just those scared kids."

"What's with that idiot?" one of the men asked. "Leaving them kids all alone is just plain stupid, fire or no fire."

"Seems strange, don't it?"

"Yup. But I've had my doubts about that one."

The fire was quickly extinguished with little damage to the building. One of the men looked around for the priest, who in his haste, had run off to the garage. He had a definite fear of fire—kids or no kids.

There had been a conflagration during a riot at the prison and he came close to being roasted alive in his cell. He was now in the habit of avoiding any sort of organized activity, having been incarcerated for so many years with other unsavory characters.

At the café, Juanita had all the kids take seats. "Where was the priest when the fire started?" she asked June.

"I don't know. He left after the first lesson. Some man came to talk to him. I never saw the man before today."

"Well, I'll be got to—oh, never mind." She called to Mindy to bring out soup and lemonade for the *almost-waifs* until their parents could be notified to pick them up.

One of the men came back from the fire cussing and raising hell.

Juanita told him to shut his trap. "You've got oral diarrhea, and in front of these kids, no less."

"Sorry. I just couldn't see that useless priest leaving these kids alone. Someone should horsewhip his ass. I mean his backside."

"That's okay. I feel the same way. I'll have Mindy re-heat your meal. It's on the house for helping out with the fire."

"Geez, thanks Juanita. I didn't expect nothing special. I'll surely enjoy it now."

*   *   *

Harry and Celeste drove up in the jeep and parked it out front. They'd been down to the river trying their luck. Other than a few mosquito bites, they didn't get a single nibble.

"You two ready for dinner yet?"

"Sure thing. What's Mindy got going tonight?"

"You're in luck. Special's beef fajitas. She might even put together a salad as a treat."

"Good deal. I'll hop back to the *necessary* and wash my paws while she puts it together," Harry said.

"Where did all the kids come from?" Celeste wanted to know.

Juanita related the fire incident. "There's just no pity for that man when the families hear about how he treated the young 'uns."

"I wouldn't want to be in *his* shoes, that's for sure. Does anyone know where he took off to?" Celeste asked.

"Not yet, but soon someone will find out, and then it's Katy bar the door."

Harry returned. After hearing of the fire, and the priest's disappearance, he said, "Soon as I eat, I have a chore to take care of. Cheri, you might want to go back to the motel and wait for me there."

"Will there be trouble, mon cher?"

She was concerned and anxious.

"If there is, I can handle it. *Pas si bête*—I'm not such a fool—I'll keep on my toes. After all, I've had years of experience in these matters, yes?"

He found reason to find polemic in her statement.

It was an hour or so after sunset when Harry made his way to the barn. He was quite certain the priest was meeting with Renaldo over something clandestine.

Chapter Twenty-Six

Timco was up early, as usual, and had the cook fire stoked up, preparing breakfast. He was in the process of making Navajo fry bread. He watched bacon sizzle in the cast-iron skillet. It brought a rush of saliva to his mouth.

"You're sure hard at it this morning," Jack croaked, not fully awake.

"Yup. The trouble with doing nothing is—you never know when you're finished. I like keeping busy."

"Sounds about right. I'll help myself to some of that coffee and leave you be."

Jack had the luxury of sleeping in later than usual. When he woke, he noticed a small nylon, two-man tent standing about twenty yards northwest of the digs. It was suppurating in the blazing sun.

It was already hellish hot.

The tent opening faced east, as was the custom with the indigenous peoples. This was intended to stop most of the wind or rain, from the west, to enter. It also allowed for the healing morning sun to enter.

The day was gobbling up time in an inescapable cycle—as it did yesterday and will do again tomorrow.

Coffee mug in hand, Jack moseyed over to the tent to check things out.

The white scut of a rabbit flashed as it fled into it's warren.
Smoke was bleeding through the brush from the interloper's fire.

An old man and a young boy were hunkered down around what smelled like a cow patty fire. The small, caramel-colored, dwarfish boy, almost stark naked, sat across the smelly fire from the wrinkled ancient one. The old one squatted on his haunches, more like a bullfrog than a man, fanning the slight flames with his ragged hat.

"How come you're camped here?" Jack demanded.

Nothing but a grunt was the old man's bilious reply.

He took a chaw of jerky and stated something to the boy.

Jack called Timco over to see if he could interpret.

The grandfather and boy spoke a strange Navajo patois—due to the fact they moved around so much. Not quite an obloquy of Indian language. It was a conglomeration of Mexican, Ute, Creek, Kiowa, Mohave, Taos, Pima, Comanche, Pecos, Arapaho, Hopi, Chiricahua, Jemez, and Zuni.

It would probably sound to the unwary Japanese in WWII like the *secret* words used by the Navajo Code Talkers.

To the uninitiated, these Athabaskan based languages sounded like nothing more than guttural gibberish—the voices of animals.

Timco spoke to the old man in a halting version of Navajo. It had been quite some time since he had to use the language. He was having difficulty contextualizing.

"Do you understand anything these two savages are saying?" Jack asked, exasperated.

The boy sprang up suddenly and walked away from the fire. He took a leak on an anthill, watching as the enemy scattered. He was practicing his aim; learning to be a warrior. He smiled broadly and returned to the fire.

"I catch the meaning of most of it," Timco answered. "Seems they were on the trail to nowhere— slowly— when they heard the road grader and decided to investigate. The sounds led them here.

"I asked about the tent and the old one explained that a tipi was too bulky and heavy for their spavined horse—ground tethered nearby. Besides, the poor animal had enough trouble moving itself, much less hauling a travois. So, they decided on a lighter refuge. The old one is a self-proclaimed shaman."

This brought a smile to the old man's lips. A twinkle to his eyes.

"I think he understands what you're saying," Jack said.

"Yes, wise one. I speak the tongue of you *new people* also, but it doesn't suit me. There are too many words."

"That's the damndest thing I've ever heard!" Jack growled.

"In our travels we have learned much. Moiety of the tribes isn't all that bad, you know. It takes the best of each to become one people. There is much anthropology in this. The language is handed down from generation to generation. Very little was ever written."

"That's all pretty hard to swallow," Jack said.

The old man poked at the fire with a piece of mesquite and continued.

"Oh, but you must believe! If you have no sense of humor you will die without a buffalo robe over your shoulders. Let me explain to you, urbanite.

"The only Indian you probably ever saw, before coming out west, was a wooden one outside a cigar store and made up to look like Sitting Bull. In fact, you city folk come out here thinking us wild Indians are still on the warpath, taking scalps. It's the truth, enit?"

"Not so, old man. I had a part Mohawk working for me at one time, but the lazy turd came to the jobsite half in the bag most of the time. I let him go after ten days."

"You say this Mohawk fella was a lazy turd. Do you know what a turd is?"

"Sure. It's a piece of shit."

"No, no, no, no, no! It's a diné derogatory label for sorcerers. From far back in time the Turds have been known to frown upon kindly, nice people. The Turds are said to be very potent and they have ways to do many bad things. You have much to learn about our Indian ways, pale one. I don't remember where I heard of this, but it makes sense."

Jack frowned in thought. "Don't you and the boy get tired of moving around all the time?"

"I don't complain," the old one answered, as he complains to the boy. "More fire! How can we cook with such a little flame?"

Jack called Timco aside and asked quietly, "Do you think we can trust those two enough to let them stay around?"

"There's good and bad Injuns, Jack, same as the general run of whites. As an example, in the past there were some wild Mescalaro Apaches. Now, they're quite subdued and live on a rez."

"I get the point. That's good enough for me."

Jack went back to the fire. "By the way, old man, how come you know so much about everything? I recall you said you and the boy moved around a lot, but you seem to have a grasp of many different things."

"I am not what I seem, pale face. Some years ago I had a dream to attend Carlisle College, where the great Jim Thorpe went. My father was strictly against me going back east even though I had good grades. I ran away from home and did odd jobs for awhile."

He raised his head and appeared to be deep in thought.

"After awhile, I found out bumming around didn't suit me either, so I went back home; apologizing to my father. He didn't take kindly to my actions. He arranged to send me to Haskell Indian Nations University in Lawrence, Kansas. That was a mistake. I only lasted two months there. The country was too flat for my liking. Ran away to take a job on a ranch in western Colorado."

"You sure must have been one nasty young man."

"Not me. I was just a free-wheeler. You sabbee?"

"Sure. I think I understand. Most young people need to rebel at some time in their life. To sow some wild oats. You think I'm stupid, or something?"

"You said it, I didn't."

"Anyhow, redskin, if you're going to stick around here bothering us, how's about a name?"

"Sure. To appease *you* only. I'm called Three Bears and the young 'un is Three Fingers. He had a minor accident aways back and lost his nose picker."

"Yeh. Right. Okay. Another thing, while I'm thinking of it, how come it takes you half a day to answer my questions? Got something to hide?"

"Not really. My theory is, never say one word when twenty or more will do."

He squinted through the smoke from their meager fire and smirked with a lopsided grin.

Jack figured it was a waste of time talking to this chronically dyspeptic person.

CHAPTER TWENTY-SEVEN

"You know, Doc, this project could go a helluva lot faster if we had more troops," Timco offered.

"I'm sure it would, but where do you find workers out here in the middle of nowhere?"

"I can solve that riddle for you, if you'll give me the okay. First, you've got to provide some way to pay wages."

"Oh, didn't I tell you? There's been a sudden influx of funds from some anonymous benefactor. He's provided sufficient funds for us to complete the project. We can go ahead full-bore now."

"That's great! I can have all the workers you need within a week to ten days. I'll take off in the morning."

"How many people do you think you can recruit? I'll want a minimum of thirty good workers."

"Don't get your balls in an uproar, Doc. I'll handle everything."

"Alright, already. I can manage to keep the students busy for a few more days. Jack's leaving for town in the morning, so that leaves me alone out here. He said he needs to make a telephone call."

"Sure. And he's also got the *hots* for one filly who needs stud service, yeh?"

"That's more than likely."

Doc wandered off in the direction of the north wall. There was a shout and some cursing from one of the workers.

"What's all that yelling about," he asked nobody in particular.

"Andoni got something in his hand and he says it hurts something fierce."

Doc strode over. "Let me take a look at the dunderhead."

He glanced but briefly.

"Hmmm. It's just a subcutaneous splinter. A slight adumbrate agitation. Cut it out with your pocket knife and swab some balm on it from that green can at the mess tent. Then get back to work! We're burning daylight!"

*   *   *

Naomi was ecstatic when she returned from her recruiting trip. She had obtained the services of the Green sisters, Red and Brown. They had been scraping by working the streets of Old Town. Naomi made them an offer they couldn't refuse.

Red Green had flaming hair. Brown Green's was more of an auburn. She never did get their proper front names, but that made no never-mind.

Brown Green was a versatile addition to the crib. She was an egalitarian hermaphrodite and could service both sexes with fervency. During slack times, Naomi took advantage of her talents and introduced her to several neglected, horny women of her acquaintance. Brown began making house calls.

The widows of the several miners, killed at the mine, were tight-lipped and word of Brown's exploits were super secret. They couldn't be forced to reveal their closeted sexual fantasies even by threat of tar and feathering.

Naomi explained to Celeste that all wasn't a bed of roses in her establishment. It seems the *segundo* of the Star-Bar ranch showed up the other day two sheets to the wind and ordered Madeline outside. She was tall, blonde, beautiful, but a rather stiff girl. He wanted a little more than what was offered.

"He was angry and speaking of *whorish women,* who he said should be allowed to roam at will and not charge for their services."

"She told him he was a repellent person and not fit to be seen in town. He was, after all, small, bowlegged, and with a short reddish beard. A real pecker head. When she said he was a little monster—that did it.

"The cowboy had an unbridled temperament. He grabbed her and threw her to the ground, kissed her, stripped her, and regardless of who was present, proceeded to violate her. I had to corral him, using a stout club of mesquite, bashing him on the head."

"Did he cause any more trouble after that?" Celeste asked, amused.

"Not hardly. I threw him over his saddle, ran his belt around the pommel, and shooed the animal away with a swat on it's arse end."

"Good for you. I bet he'll pass the word around not to mess with Naomi, huh?"

"He by God better if he knows what's good for his ornery hide."

CHAPTER TWENTY-EIGHT

"When do we noon?" the gangly student asked. He was practically bent over double with hunger pains.

"No such a time on this project. When the boss stops, we stop. He's got a time machine in his gut that nudges him to eat—which isn't all that often."

It was but a short time later that Doc called a halt to the digging. He motioned for Timco to join him at the four by eight piece of plywood; their temporary table. A large sheet of butcher paper lay on it, anchored by stones at the corners. They squatted over it like a pair of magpies.

"Our best way to dig is to draw up a ground plan using the readings we took with the magnetometers," Doc surmised.

They had utilized two fluxgate types to define the pueblo outline. It appeared that gestalt connections were absent. "Those flags we planted are only a general scheme of the whole," Doc explained, as he sketched the outline of the digs. "I'll take a couple of those Herculean-looking youths with me to the north wall."

The remaining standing portion of the wall had served as a sheep corral at one time—a crop and drop area.

"Ruth Golden Eagle can take the center area, where the kiva should be located, and you, my aborigine companion, can begin work with the two remaining scholars near that outgrowth over there," he said, gesturing to the east.

"Why me?"

"Because I think you have an instinct for wild, untamed Indian relics."

"Go to hell, Doc!"

Ignoring the outburst, he insisted in his tirade. "I also believe you're under the misconception that Don Ameche invented the telephone, without which your people would still be communicating with tom-toms and smoke signals."

"What he hell do you mean by *my people?*" Timco barked.

"Well, you're one of those aborigine heathens, aren't you?"

"Listen here, you *almost* bald Anglo—," He gritted his teeth.

"There's no need for us to criticize that which is a known fact, Timco. Let's let bygones be bygones and get back to the task at hand, shall we? Just consider my slight insult a bagatelle."

"Whatever you say, egg-head."

Timco wasn't satisfied. The argument seemed to go Doc's way, as usual. What the hell was a bagatelle?

Ruth Golden Eagle didn't seem to care, one way or another, that she was relegated to the center section. When informed, her ochre brow furrowed slightly above an almost stoic face.

There was complete silence as she led her two workers to the site.

Doc was becoming irritated by the young people's profligacy. He never-the-less beamed with benignity upon his *children*. They were learning fast.

Meanwhile, Erdu proceeded to bang on a pot with gusto, signifying that lunch was ready.

There was an immediate stampede to the kitchen area. "Eat your fill and get back to work post-haste," Doc admonished.

"Why the big rush, Doc? The pueblo isn't going anywhere." Timco said. "Besides, I'll get those extra hands here in a jiffy."

"Simply because man spends as much time excreting as he does eating, and I'm sure there'll be a detour to the outhouse for most of them."

"You know, Doc, you can be a real hard-nose sometimes. If you were a Duke or something, I'd call you a royal pain in the ass."

CHAPTER TWENTY-NINE

Jack was only a short way out of camp when he came upon Mike lounging on the grader, apparently taking a break. Having sat idle too long near Naomi's place, the yellow paint on the Caterpillar grader was pitted and sand-blasted by storms.

He reined in and asked if there was any trouble.

"Not so's you'd notice. Just getting' a second wind."

"Okay. I'll be riding on then."

Mike had a fair to middling landscaper's eye. The road ran between two large yuccas. They formed a gateway of sorts to the campsite.

"If you be riden' back to town on the road, keep your eye out for Cliff in one of his rigs. He'll be haulin' the makings of a modular. He drives like a bat outta hell, you know."

"I'll do that. Thanks."

He noticed that Mike was being careful to keep one side of his face partially hidden; out of the sun. A quick glance revealed that a rash had begun on his left cheek. It might be embarrassing so he didn't mention it.

A mile further on, the well-graded portion of the road crossed a small wash. It was dried up, flowing with nothing but small rocks and pebbles that had been rounded and smoothed from the time when there was water that licked them and then left them behind.

In town he left the horse with Alfredo and made straight for Agnes's house. Her good humor and healthy natural appetite had an obvious effect on him. Since neither wished to be led to the altar, they got along very well, meeting when the urge took them—never under duress.

For the many years of his marriage to Ruth, he had been uxorious, but he was beginning to have strong feelings for Agnes, just not as a bed mate. Yet, as with most men, his penis determined the directed course of action.

Following a quick roll in the hay, he said, "Let's make a trip over to the cantina. I'm as dry as an eight-day camel and can only piss dust."

"You always seem to say the most endearing things to me, Jack. How can a woman refuse? Anyhow, you're acting like a bull elk in rut. I'm not sure I can keep up. Take a breath now and then."

"That bad, huh? Sorry about that. You realize, of course, we've been apart for over two weeks and I think we're both a bit wanton."

"That's some smart-ass answer, but it'll have to do for now. Climb into your trousers, and let's go see Han Po."

The evening crowd hadn't shown up as yet. One lone cowboy was leaning back in his chair, sombrero-styled hat tilted over his face. A half-empty bottle of cerveza sat on the table, drawing flies.

The place smelled of spit and sweat and cigars and horses and cow chips someone must have stepped in. The swamper was lax in his duties this day.

"Hey there, Han Po, how's the old hammer hanging?" Jack shouted.

"Just like eighteen pounds of swinging meat, you rascal, you. I thought maybe you'd left the territory."

"Not hardly. Been out with Doc on the digs. Keeping busy."

"That's good. I see you brought along your backup in case of trouble. Good-day, Agnes. Should I bring you a drink, or do you have to wait for Mister Tightwad to cough up some loot?"

"Never mind him, Han Po, I have my own money. You can make it two. I'll break down and treat the poor beast. He's all sunburned and dried out."

"What a fine gesture for one so genteel. I might even treat you both. It's been a quiet day with no one to talk to. You'll have to do for now." He chuckled. "My only other customer is acting like a mortician's cadaver and won't even glance my way."

"Seems like I've seen him around somewhere," Jack said.

"That may be. Enough prattle. Let me bring cold drinks for you thirsty Arabs. You must have walked over as I don't see your camels tied outside."

"You got that right. We rode shank's mare."

"Did I hear you say you were out at the digs?" the cowboy said, suddenly coming to life.

"That's right. What about it?"

"Just curious. They say you folks are digging for Spanish treasure."

"Is that what they say? Guess they've been smoking that funny stuff. Isn't anything out there but dirt as far as I can tell."

The cowboy shifted his hat back on his forehead. His porcine eyes were drilling holes through the dust motes and smoky haze. It didn't seem to matter what Jack said to him. He had his mind made up.

"I'll be saying adios, Han Po and the same to you, friend. Be seein' ya around."

"What's all that about?" Agnes asked, as the cowboy made tracks.

"Beats me. He might be thinking of robbing us of some mesquite bushes down the road. Who knows?"

"Just be careful out there," Han Po warned. "Too many people are out of work and it won't take too much to sneak out there and steal what they can get their hands on."

"No problem. We've got that killer dog, Midnight, and Timco keeps a shotgun within reach at all times."

CHAPTER THIRTY

Mike struggled the short distance into camp with considerable effort. He was feeling crappy. Been vomiting, shaking, and had chills.

The rash became quite painful. Red and swollen with the consistency of an orange peel. There wasn't time to dwell on it. He needed medical help—soon.

Doc took one quick look and escorted him to the Quonset. Although only partially completed, it would serve as a temporary shelter until Cliff arrived with the truck.

Within the hour, a cloud of red dust chasing him, Cliff swerved into position to unload.

"Cliff!" Doc yelled over the roar of the truck's engine. "Take everyone and unload in a quick-ass hurry. We've got a medical emergency here and I need you to haul Mike into the hospital with haste. He's got some weird sort of disease working on his skin."

"Is it contagious?"

"I don't think so, but try not to get too near him. We can rig up some sort of pad in the bed of the truck for him to lay on. That way you won't have to touch him."

"Okay. Let's get this stuff unloaded. I'll play alligator and haul ass getting him to the hospital. Just hope he's not too far gone."

The unloading went rapidly.

Cliff made excellent time into the hospital. They immediately placed Mike in the isolation ward. By now the infection had spread over the entire left side of his face.

It was determined that he had developed the symptoms of Erysipelas. People with a history of alcoholism, of which Mike was afflicted at one time, are considered at increased risk.

Most cases of Erysipelas are due to *Streptococcus pyogenes*—also known as Group A streptococci. Mike was now in a critical stage of the illness and probably contacted it several days ago, unbeknownst to him. The doctors placed him on a strong treatment of intravenous antibiotics.

After insuring everything medically possible was being done, Cliff left, with his solemn promise to return the next day.

The news wasn't all that good when he showed up with Doc and Ernie in tow, and a large box of chocolates. "Didn't know what else to bring," he apologized.

While the doctor was explaining the situation, Ernie began to eat several pieces of chocolate, avoiding the caramel-filled ones. They stuck to his partial plate.

"What the hell are you doin', Ernie? That chocolate is for Mike, you dingbat!"

"Just testing to see if it's fresh."

"You realize, of course, that stuff is an aphrodisiac? You'll be as horny as a dog in heat before we leave here," Doc chided.

"Say what? That I don't need!" he moaned, and put a half-eaten piece back in the box. "Since the old lady died, I've been on the sex wagon."

"Lot's of luck. You're hooked now, that's for sure."

*　　*　　*

As Yellow Fox rode across the wold on his piebold horse, he espied a *chiindii*—a dust devil. It was rotating in a clockwise direction.

A good sign.

Advance word of his arrival was being passed on the wind; the magical Indian telegraph. One Yellow Fox of the Diné was recruiting workers for a dig at a new-found pueblo. It was incumbent on those approached to join this religious endeavor. The previous inhabitants were now the ghosts of past relatives, after all.

The recruited Indians trekked along slowly beneath an angry sun, making for the canyon, and eventually their campsite at the digs.

It was a magnificent caravan. Young, old and many in between. Horses, dogs. goats and few mules carrying household goods. Some people were chanting and some were chatting, some were laughing and some were giggling—telling lies and stories of bravery and other exploits.

They strode along purposely to the accompaniment of drums, heedless of the uneven terrain.

An eagle flew across their path—seeing which, an old man, beaming with joy, in his superstitious belief, cried out with delight, "Ah, look at that good omen! Now our journey will be certain to prove worthy."

Four young men were sent ahead to procure water for the tired, thirsty travelers who were bivouacked four day's march away in a large arroyo that provided some partial shade.

CHAPTER THIRTY-ONE

It was beginning to get dark when Harry arrived at the barn. There was a light showing beneath the door next to Jack's storage room. Jack's key was in his pocket. He opened the lock and let himself into the space as quietly as possible. The door resisted. He was wearing dark clothes and soft-soled shoes.

The voices were very distinct, which pleased him. It would make it easier to differentiate between individuals. there were six men in all, and the obvious leader was the so-called priest, who asked if there had been any trouble at the border.

"Oh, no! We paid the usual *La Mordida* to those lazy patrolmen along the border and we came right through."

"Where's the other two men?"

"As you told us, compadre, if those people don't behave we were to kill them, yes? They met with terrible accidents."

The priest clucked his tongue, displaying a spurious remorse. He was, after all, an actor by nature.

"How much did you manage to get through this time?"

"A bit over forty-five kilos."

"So where's the stuff from those two who met their end?"

"Sorry, amigo. We had to leave it. The Federalies were close by."

"You bunch of numb-nuts! Don't you realize that's almost two-hundred grand laying around in the desert? Cold, hard cash right out of *my* pocket! I should kill the lot of you right now!" he menaced, waving a pistol.

"Por favor. Waving that pistola makes me nervous."

"Shut your face, Renaldo. I'll damned well wave it any time I feel like it. I might start using it too."

He squinted at the four culprits.

"Leaving those goods out there is against the rules. You damned will know that, don't you? Leaving the bodies makes me no never mind, but *never* leave the goods!" he scowled. "If I don't decide to take it out on your hides, I'll sure as hell deduct it from your shares!"

While the haranguing was taking place, Harry made his way out of the room quietly. Once outside, he took a deep breath to clear his head. That so-called priest is a complete shit; corrupt, incompetent, with a bit of cunning. Also, he was quite unconcerned in regard those two couriers laying dead, who without them, his profits dwindled immensely.

He was an evil man, heading an evil enterprise.

Harry retraced his steps back to the cantina. A drink would do his psyche a world of good.

*　　*　　*

Heat lightning scythed the night sky off to the west. A threatening storm had stayed away, tracking northeast. Snatches of thunder, stolen from the storm, rumbled like kettle drums, finally dissipating quietly as though involved in the climax of a Wagner opera.

He rapped loudly on the sturdy old wooden door of the vicarage. Movement was heard within.

"Who's out there bothering me at this un-godly hour?"

"Open up mister, or I'll be forced to smash down the door!"

"It's you again! The insurrectionist! You can go straight to hell!"

"That would suit me fine, mon amie. I would be certain to meet you there, and I wouldn't have to stand out here in the dark, like some fool, waiting for you to unlatch the door."

The man was in a sullen, spiteful mood as he yanked at the sturdy door, leaving it only partially open.

Harry pushed it to it's full extent. He could see the priestly one had moved back into the room.

He advanced on the obscenely scrofulous person.

"Do you really expect to continue your dirty operations here? It's bad enough that you pretend to be a man of God, but when you and your vermin cohorts distribute that nasty stuff for monetary gain, I put my foot down!"

"You mention God. Is the world around us created by God? Or, did man invent God? We must be either in heaven or hell. Think about that, mister!"

"I've decided there's a place for your twisted mind to be at ease. There's an old story that goes something like this: In the crypt of the abbey church in Vasilmio, the monks were boiling their bishop. When the townspeople heard about it, they came en masse and burned the church down around the monks."

"So what does that little story tell *me?* he sneered.

"Just that when this little town hears about your shenanigans, you could possibly end up with a fate worse than death. It was bad enough how you treated the kids. You probably already figured out I don't care for you or your kind, being the smart ass you are. I'm going to do my damndest to run you out of business, mon ami."

He paused for a moment, expecting some rebuttal. When none was forthcoming, he continued.

"It will come to pass, mah fren', that you will be the last in line. You'll see. When the people of the town find you out, beware! They all know that good is good and you are the devil!"

Then, with an expressive shrug, he said, "I'm rather surprised you would have the audacity to think those priest's clothes would make you a true believer. It takes a whole lot more than that to cleanse that wicked soul of yours."

The priest's dark eyes had a wild glint.

He rummaged among several bottles on the sideboard, accidentally overturning one. He poured himself a stiff drink of bourbon. From across the room, Harry caught the odor of the man. Along with the stench of stagnant perspiration, there was the strong smell of a distillery, quite offensive to the nostrils.

Harry left the priest swilling on the bottle.

As he stepped outside he looked up at the heavens and thought there were too many stars for the sky. It appeared to be top-heavy.

*   *   *

In the café the next morning, Jack pulled a chair up to Harry and Celeste's table.

"Have you found out anything with your snooping yet?"

"Some strangers have been around the garage and there's been lots of activity at night. I have that Indian policeman—what's his name?"

"Cooper."

"That's him. I've got him on alert and he's been contacting some buddies in DEA. We could be coming up with something real soon."

"That's great! I knew you were a genuine Mike Hammer type when I first met you."

"Don't get too carried away, Jack. It's just something I did for many years and it comes easy for me."

He leaned closer to Jack and cupped a hand alongside his mouth, so that he could relay some information quietly, in a felicitous manner. A discretion, perhaps, but necessary in light of the subject matter and those in attendance.

"You must keep me informed of that so-called priest's bowel movements. His are bound to be sporadic—he's so full of shit."

"I'll do that, Harry," he said with a narrow eyed smile.

CHAPTER THIRTY-TWO

Doc was in a real dither. Now that Mike was invalid and the road wasn't ready, it grated on him that the project may be delayed indefinitely. It wasn't as though he didn't have some feelings for Mike, it was just that things were going so well—and now.

He approached Jack explaining his dilemma.

"What's the big deal, Doc? If that grader's got a motor, some gears and enough fuel, I'll give it a whirl. I used to run a fork lift and a crane on my jobs so I can sure as hell figure out how to run *that* monster."

"Are you sure? I wouldn't want to have you injured, along with Mike. We're running behind schedule as it is."

Doc was about concerned with Jack's welfare as a tortoise worries about beating the hare. The project was number one priority. Doc was all heart.

Jack climbed aboard the yellow monster, as he called it, and proceeded to check out the workings. Not too difficult, he decided.

The pueblo site was on a slight rise from where he now sat, up the canyon a mile or so.

The immense canyon, formed by some ancient river eons ago, was enclosed by sandstone walls that reached for the sky some two-hundred feet or more.

Found in the sandstone were fossils of shells and fish vertebrae, encased when the whole area was covered in a vast ocean which ran from present day northern Mexico to near the Utah border, during pre-Permian times.

Although most of the territory within the canyon was now quite arid, here and there were small pools, left from rains many miles away that temporarily inundated it with torrents of water.

These miniature pools were home to small frogs and water beetles that skated on the surface, apparently the only living creatures for miles.

Progress along the marked boundaries of the road was quite easy. The grader scraped away dead cactus residue, mesquite bushes and small boulders with ease. Mike had managed a good job of delineating the outlines of the road, providing Jack with an excellent path to follow.

On his second day at the job, the long, noisy procession passed by. The group was in good spirits, anticipating cool water and a hot meal. They would be greeted by Yellow Fox. He had made up three large pots of slumgullion from several captured jackrabbits and whatever vegetables he could scrounge from the larder.

*   *   *

Toothless Dragonfly, with her large, sad, black eyes that bulged slightly, presided over the conglomeration of humans and animals. She was rather corpulent, but carried it well. She was a lovely woman. Love seeped out through her pores to envelop everyone around her. Her neatly tied hair was as black and shiny as licorice.

She called Jack 'Twoon Powa because of his well-formed face and dark hair. She'd seen an old movie, *The Mark of Zorro*, starring the original Tyrone Power, and considered the resemblance close enough.

Dragonfly was a schemer, that's for sure.

Her first demand was for higher wages for the women, who, she emphatically stated, were the hardest workers. It was known that the men were somewhat slovenly and lazy and wont to take on minor chores or take off hunting on a whim. Her pay scale submitted to Doc was suitably approved: $1.75/hr. for women; $1.50/hr. for men; $1.00/hr. for teens; children twelve and under $3.00/day.

These monies were a god-send to all involved and would help to get them out of the depression-type living conditions they were experiencing on the rez.

The woman was already forty-two years old when she was born and now numbered so many years people thought she would never die. She was far beyond being an octogenarian. Doc installed her as the record keeper and pay clerk, she being the senior member of the group. It would be her duty to dole out the daily wages and assign duties. It had been determined on other digs that Doc was involved with, that payment daily kept the workers happy and prevented mutiny.

The workers shared an easily wounded sensibility, quick to detect the slightest changes—and to suffer from them. Even the lowliest one, senses the breathing of a great organism. They were all aware that the further one goes up the hierarchy the easier it is to get lost. A strict leader is necessary to accomplish the assigned tasks.

Dragonfly understood how urgent it was to obey orders from above and then to relay those orders in an understanding way to her minions, who had left their homes in search of suitable work.

She was also aware of the necessity of maintaining a daily record of accomplishments, not only for the dispersal of wages, but for the historical aspects of the project.

When notified a barracks-style building would be erected for the people, she rebelled in a vociferous manner. Dragonfly was very superstitious. She immediately ordered a *tsé bee hooghan*—a circular female Hogan—to be built in a place or her choosing. She had an aversion to square rooms claiming the spirits invaded those structures and would hide in the corners.

Her forefathers told of those spirits, and she believed.

The Hogan is considered sacred to those who practice the Navajo religion. The circular female Hogan is the family home for the diné peoples. In it, the children play, the women cook, weave, talk and entertain and the men tell jokes and stories.

The doorway of the Hogan would face east, as is prescribed.

The religious song, *The Blessingway,* describes the first Hogan as being built by Coyote with help from beavers. The Beaver People gave Coyote logs and instructions on how to build it.

As was usual when dealing with the indigenous peoples, Yellow Fox would be the intermediary, squelching any doubts from the two-legged white people. With some little reservation, Doc went along with all his decisions.

Once the Indians had been fed, and their camp set up, they prepared the area for a celebration by building a huge bonfire in the center. On cue, there was a beating of drums, ululations and stomping of bare feet upon the earth. Some of the dancers wore small bells on their ankles providing a tinkling accompaniment.

A thrilling display of horsemanship had everyone cheering. A checkered flag, waved briskly by a youngster, announced the end of the event.

This was soon followed by a rousing tomahawk contest among some young men. Targets were set up against two small cedars. A required skill for the competitors was evident. Some of the tomahawks were as heavy as thirty-five pounds and up to thirty-six inches in length.

The drums were thrumming once more.

Obviously, Doc wasn't too impressed with these displays of athleticism. "Are you enjoying this characteristic covetousness of the aboriginal, Timco?"

"Beats the hell out a minuet, Doc," he managed with a straight face.

A group of children broke away from the festivities and began chanting, "Ashes, ashes, all fall down." Like small children everywhere, Indian children love to play. Children who grow up together, learn together, share life's pleasures and pain together, and become long friends.

Later they joined in song. A song, sung by small children, is enchanting and full of life. It penetrates the ear, the heart, the soul.

The adults release a soft sigh and enjoy the music.

Memories.

Doc was invited to join some elders for their meal. Yellow Fox would act as majordomo, ensuring all went well.

Doc's attitude didn't help matters.

To partially appease him, Timco laced his coffee with a stop-gap shot of brandy in lieu of his usual sugar ration.

Naturally, Dragonfly took him under her wing, he being the senior *white eyes* present.

"You must eat healthy, nourishing food—less meat. All white man's food is over-sugared and over-salted. That leaves no natural taste."

The food was presented. Doc grimaced. It consisted of items called the *three sisters*. It wasn't exactly steak and lobster. Actually, it was roasted rattler, baked squash, two kinds of beans, corn and fry bread.

The repast was placed in the center of the group. There was a whir of arms and hands that engulfed Doc. The lady sitting next to him smiled broadly and stated, "When one eats with the Indian, one must have long arms and a trained diet, yes?"

"What? No pemmican?" he asked sarcastically.

"Oh, no! That is for the trail only, silly man!"

She slapped his hand gently and began to pray for the bounty received.

Later he was entertained for almost an hour with amusing fables. Then the calumet was passed. It was made from pipe stone, a type of carvable rock.

They smoked in silence.

"I hope you enjoyed your evening, Doc," Dragonfly asked. "Hospitality lives only one day."

A lugubrious howl broke the silence. The sound, eerie in the night, tendered fear in the young ones. In the light of the full moon the source was seen as a bitch albino coyote, standing on an outcrop just beyond the campsite.

Albinos are crepuscular animals that lack camouflage and are unable to conceal themselves from prey. Survival rate is low.

"Just an overgrown dog," Doc murmured.

"Scoff, you learned one," Timco admonished. "The ancient ones revered white as a symbol. It's a symbol of peace, purity, innocence, happiness, joy and virginity. The Indians gave a white belt of wampum as a pledge of honor; it reflected the benignity of age; white typifies the majesty of justice in the ermine of a judge's garb; to the noble Iroquois, the midwinter sacrifice of the sacred *White Dog,* a holiest of festivals."

He paused to scratch his ass and let the information sink in.

"So you see, Doc, that albino coyote is an amazing specimen of nature, and showing itself should be taken as an omen."

"Maybe so, but it's still just a bunch of myths you're talking about."

"Of course, but in a deeply tribal sense we love our myths."

The experience of the albino coyote was a time out of sync.

*   *   *

It was after the ceremonies.

There were many tipi's, some small camp tents and many bodies spread over the ground, some in sleeping bags.

They all slept.

Some slept as if crucified, legs and arms spread-eagled.

They slept in flurries, snoring, panting and puffing.

There would be no escape for the sleepers until morning.

Not so!

"Eeeeyah!"

A scream filled the air, coming from the encampment.

Timco raced there, half asleep, trying to discover the source of this intrusion to his dreams. Other than some mumblings from nearby tents, he was on the prowl solo.

A young maiden was standing outside her tent, hugging herself, eyes wide with fright, pleading for help.

An enlarged shadow of a tarantula had appeared on the side of her tent; projected there by the campfire.

Evidently a male species was wandering around seeking a mate.

Timco smiled briefly.

"It's only a spider," he explained. "I know it's quite ugly looking, but it won't bother you. In fact, they can be trained as pets. Even if it does bite it will only sting for a little while and then itch like a mosquito bite."

She didn't appear to believe him.

"I'll tell you what. Let me pick it up and show you I won't be bothered. It will lay in my hand nice and quiet."

He reached down and gathered the large, hairy, eight-eyed spider softly into his open palm. "See? Not a bit of trouble. Now, why don't you go back to bed and try to get some sleep."

"It's still a scary thing," she shrugged.

"It may be, but you don't have to worry any more tonight. I'll move it out of the camp so it won't bother anyone else, okay?"

"That's good. Thank you."

"You're more than welcome, little one."

Others who had been awakened listened to Timco with one ear, and with the other to erotic enterprises of their neighbors.

It seems the disturbances weren't over yet. Three students took it upon themselves to ambuscade the compound, whacking on the sides of several tents and yelling, "Get up and piss, the world's on fire!"

Their rampage lasted but a few moments.

This was to cause no end of consternation among the inhabitants. Before a war party could be assembled, Timco sent the intruders back to their quarters with a warning, and then appeased those in camp who had been bothered.

"What next?" [he wondered] as Venus, in all it's brilliance, appeared in the east. He was about to give up on any further rest for this night. There was probably a reason the ancients called Venus *Lucifer*.

CHAPTER THIRTY-THREE

"Where are all those people going to take a crap?" Jack asked, with some concern.

Timco pointed southeast and held his thumb and forefinger closely together, indicating a short distance.

They walked in that direction and came upon a small ravine giving off the aroma of an overflowing cesspool.

"At least they considered the prevailing winds from the northwest and used this area," Timco managed, holding back bile while pinching his nose.

"We'll have to do something about this disaster, that's for sure," Jack said.

After only a few days the stench of the effluvium was already beyond unbearable.

"They're mostly clean people and didn't want to defile their living area," Timco explained.

"When Cliff shows up, I'll ask him to pick up some quicklime and two or three more chemical outhouses. The two we now have aren't nearly enough. They're being overused. Always a line two-deep waiting," Jack informed him.

"You think maybe Doc will have something to say about that?"

"I don't much care. Anyhow, he's too busy daydreaming about what he's going to find after we uncover the pueblo."

"There goes Midnight in the direction of the ravine. Ever notice that when a dog needs to dump he never needs to wipe his arse with paper like humans? His sphincter muscles close him up tight as a drum when he's done, and the he's good to go. Midnight's one well-behaved canine, that's for sure."

"Yep. That's for sure," Jack agreed and wandered off to confer with Doc.

*　　*　　*

The Morgans arrived. Harry and Celeste in the saddles. The jenny trailed behind some considerable distance, Han Po navigating her.

Han Po shifted his hat back on his forehead and stated disgustedly, *"Ren fú yú she'*—Too many people and not enough work!" when he saw all the idle bodies standing around waiting for orders.

"I shall talk to that Doctor person and straighten things out! We came out here to help, did we not?" he asked Harry.

"That we did!" Harry answered with enthusiasm. "By the way, what are you going to do about all your customers?"

"Fornicate them all!" Han Po replied in a light mood. "They will manage. That problem is in the hands of Estelle. She has orders to maintain a strict no-nonsense business. I'm sure my bartender will squeal on her if something is out of line."

Celeste was frowning. "Harry, look at all those poor tykes. I feel sorry for them."

They were a rag-tag looking bunch, for certain. They seemed to be well fed, but were clothed in hand-me-downs, most of which fit poorly.

Timco overheard this and allowed himself a slight, crooked smile.

"Poverty doesn't give them time to grow old. Actually, they're all pretty happy. Living like they do on the rez, miles from anything resembling civilization, they find things to do to keep busy and haven't any idea what it means to be without."

"That's a horrible way to grow up."

"Maybe so, Celeste, but there's very little help offered from the State or Federal Government. The parents live mostly off the land, growing a few crops and tending little herds of sheep. A small percentage have gotten an education and work in some trade."

Timco glanced away, a far-off look in his eyes, remembering his own terrible childhood.

CHAPTER THIRTY-FOUR

The workers were assembled, mumbling in several dialects, and awaited assignments. Heard among the gathered was an olio of New Mexican languages—Na Dené, Kiowa-Apache, Chiricahua, Mescalero, Jicarilla, Lipan and Navajo. Never-the-less, they were all using sign language fluently.

"Timco, I'll have you separate these people into manageable groups since you seem to understand most of them, " Doc advised.

The cant of Indian words stunned him.

"Sure, but who's going to take care of the kitchen area? I've got things started for the noon meal already."

"Don't fret about that. Pick out two or three women and let that twin you have working for you tell them what needs to be done."

"You act like it's an easy job to feed this small army, Doc. I'll have you know it's a study in logistics just to plan meals ahead," Timco groused.

"Get off your high horse. Soon as the groups have been put to work you can return to your culinary chores. I figure groups of ten, with Ruth Golden Eagle in overall charge, will do nicely."

"Nicely, huh? If you say so. I'll take one group over to that rise on the east side and get them started. Should keep Harry, Celeste and Han

Po with me. That way at least they'll understand what's required. With so much territory to cover, it might be wise for you to work the north wall. That way we can check out progress against the preliminary plot, okay?"

"That sounds reasonable. I also noticed the cliff near the north wall has some inscriptions on it. I'll give a few youngsters brushes so they can clean them up and maybe make some rubbings. Might turn out to be interesting."

"Okay. Let's get this show on the road. We're wasting time standing around batting the breeze. Whatcha doin' over there, Andoni?"

"Thinkin.'"

He was staring out across the compound trying to conjure up important thoughts, his mouth set in a sad rictus.

"That's good. Keeps the brain from rustin' up. Anyhow, this here's a working party, enit? Put your ass in gear and follow me."

The only thing Andoni was guilty of was being led by the nose by his brother, Edur, into situations he couldn't get free from. He couldn't think clearly standing on his feet—he was a perfect pawn—capable of moving only one agonizing step at a time.

*　　*　　*

"Hey, redskin! Hydrate me!"

"Say what?"

"Get me some water, dumb ass. Don't you understand English?"

"Get your own damned water, pale face!"

The young Indian reached for bespectacled Ralph's crotch and squeezed.

"No balls!" he yelled in glee.

"No balls, huh? I got gall stones biggerin' *your* balls you queer looking fag."

He raised a gnarled fist and whacked the young Indian alongside his ear, sending him sprawling over in the dirt in agony, an amazed look on his face.

"You hit hard, four eyes," he whined.

"When you get up I'll give you what fer if you don't straighten out."

The glasses were a rather cunning cover-up to Ralph's prowess.

Laying in the dirt the Indian boy didn't know how to extricate himself, peacefully, in front of his friends. He raised up slowly and said he was sorry.

Ralph slammed the boy's shoulder with the palm of his hand.

"Sorry doesn't begin to make up for your stupidity."

The boy was turning red with embarrassment.

"Don't push me again."

He flexed his fingers at his sides, closing them into a fist. He looked around and saw that his friends out-numbered the whites.

"I'll push you anytime I damned-well please," Ralph threatened.

He gut punched the boy.

He wasn't expecting the blow. It doubled him up. He grabbed his stomach, choking.

One of the students who was a wannabe Indian, stepped in front of Ralph.

"Hell, man, it ain't worth the misery to be pounding that kid and skinin' your knuckles, and maybe makin' his face look like pulp. His face is ugly enough anyhow, ain't it?"

Suddenly Timco was in the center of the action. He held both combatants at arms length.

"It seems to me the odds are a bit unfair, boys. Ralph here, outweighs the other boy by twenty-five or thirty pounds. Now then, since you both have so much extra energy, grab shovels and follow me. We'll uncover the whole pueblo in jig time, with an hour to spare."

He smiled with a reckless display of white teeth.

Midnight circled the group, yapping in glee. He thought all the commotion was part of a game. When the action came to a halt, he went back to his usual haunt near the kitchen area and laid down in the shade. Can't rely on humans for too much fun.

*   *   *

"Jayzus!" Timco screamed. "What in hell is all that racket over by the north wall?"

It seems that Doc had rigged up his tape deck, hooked it to two immense speakers, and was playing something he considered work-incentive music. The tapes were by Vivaldi, Tschaikowsky, Mozart and Rimski-Korsakow. The music was getting negative results.

Many of the workers stood around covering their ears, grimacing; preparing to strike.

"Very well, you aborigine heathens, see if you can work to this beat!"

He slipped selections of the Beatles and Beach Boys into the machine. There was an immediate attitude adjustment. Shovels, picks and buckets flew around the worksite as though caught up in a tornado.

CHAPTER THIRTY-FIVE

Jack was saddling up one of the Morgans when Three Fingers approached him. "Heading out to somewheres?"

"Yeh. Trouble with doing nothing—you never know when you're done. I've got a few things to take care of in town. It beats standing around here picking my nose."

"*Hoka Hey*, eh, Jack? That is the truth. I can understand your anxiety. I used to be that way when the moon was full. Don't stay away too long or I'll forget what your face looks like."

"Not to worry. Be gone maybe two, three days."

"That is good. *Ki ya mani yo*—recognize everything as you ride, pilgrim."

*   *   *

It was another hot, dusty day. He slip-knotted the reins to the rail and entered the café with hopes of finding Cliff inside.

No such luck.

His truck was parked nearby. He must be around town.

The sidewalk in front of the mercantile was a bastion of crates and boxes as if to ward off marauding Apaches. He went inside and found Eva scribbling in her notebook, as usual.

"Where's your broom, Eva?"

"Huh?"

"Don't you usually ride around town on it to save shoe leather?"

"Go to hell, Mr. Collins!"

Next stop was the cantina. Outside, a man dressed in cowboy attire crouched against the adobe wall, his almost-a-Stetson hat was pulled down to rest on the bridge of his nose, preventing the glaring mid-day sun from scorching the retina's of his dark, aquiline-looking eyes.

As Jack neared, he pushed his hat up an inch or two. His head turned mockingly a little to one side. He was smiling. It was an insincere smile. He was smiling with his mouth but not with his eyes.

Could he really trust this person? He had an aversion to people that wouldn't look you in the eye when they talked.

Something to hide?

His get-up also didn't add up. New jeans, shirt and boots. A lousy disguise if he ever saw one.

Forget him!

Back to the café after an interlude of about a half hour searching the town, he saw Naomi sitting in one of Juanita's thirty-minute chairs—so-called because they were just uncomfortable enough to discourage patrons from staying too long after finishing their meal.

Cliff was now inside, sitting tilted back in his chair, staring at a cold cup of coffee.

"What's up Jack? Didn't expect to see you in town for a few more days."

"Been chasing you all over town. I've got a request."

He laid out his plan quietly, as though the place was alive with customers, notwithstanding gossipy Eva.

"Sure, Jack. I can handle that for you. How soon?"

"I'll let you know. Anyhow, your next run into the city how about loading up three or four more of those chemical outhouses and some quicklime. We've got a bunch of open-bottomed Indians out there, and it's starting to smell like every sewer in the state is backing up."

"Can do. Doc gave me a big list of chow he wants me to grab at the commodity depot, and I'm planning on bringing Mike back with me. We'll also drag along a water trailer."

"Sounds good. See you later. Gotta hit the mercantile."

"Hey there, Don, I have a short list for you."

He jerked a thumb toward the front door. What's with all that stuff piled up outside?"

"Hell, with all the activity out at Doc's digs I figured I'd best get ahead of the game and stock up. There's all kinda strangers taking up space in town and Large Ruby has enough reservations to last her a month or more. Word's getting around the digs might end up being a major project."

"That could be. Say, there's this guy hanging around looking like some kinda vagabond. Been in here? He's dressed in a wrangler outfit, of sorts."

"Yup, fella answering that description came in and bought up some flour, bacon and a few other items, like he might be setting up camp hereabouts."

"He say anything to you?"

"Not a peep. Tight-lipped sort. A real jasper if I ever saw one."

He stretched his suspenders with his right thumb as though to emphasize his importance.

"I manage to keep up with the goings-on around here and report such things to officer Cooper. He thanked me and said to keep an eye out."

"Good deal, Don."

Don's partially gray hair straggled over his forehead as he turned to the rear of the store.

Jack's eyes roved away, full of anxiety. This could be more inside information to relay to Harry.

*   *   *

He walked the two short blocks to Agnes's house, ducking under her sad clothesline.

He knocked.

"Who's there?"

"It's me, Jack. Open up before I huff and puff and blow the house down, as the wolf said."

"You damned idiot!"

She dragged him forcefully, steering him to the bed. Due to the heat of her body his underwear spontaneously combusted. Or so it seemed.

A few minutes later, after catching his breath, he said, "Agnes, you're insatiable. Are you sure your husband died from uranium dust?"

"That's what they tell me."

She reached for him again, but he rolled aside.

"What's the matter, big boy, can't take it?"

"Just out of practice. How's about we hit the cantina and revive me?"

"Okay, if you insist. Be ready in a minute. Once you've been refueled, be ready for a wrestling match."

Ruby was sitting alone.

"Let's join her. She looks like she could use some company," Jack suggested.

"Good idea."

"Hi there, Large," Jack managed without being too familiar. "Nice to see you. I've got a message from that guy, Doc. Said he would be in town within three days, and to keep a light on. Has to make a few phone calls."

"That figures. Those damned digs come first with that one, you know."

"Oh, it's not all that bad, is it? He speaks often of you."

"Yeh, well, you might mention to him he owes me for the rented animals and his room. I had to move his stuff to my quarters. Needed the space."

"I figure he'll be in to settle all debts about the time I get back out there, so you can tell him yourself. Anyway, you must have time to spare, sitting around here like this."

"Motel's full, but I found me a gem of a housekeeper. She's fast. She can change sheets without even waking a customer."

Jack ordered another round.

The more time he spent around Ruby, the more he enjoyed her

company. She was a delight. Knowledgeable on many subjects and with an open sense of humor.

Sitting at the table with a toothpick dangling from her mouth, cracking her knuckles—not missing a beat in a story she was relating—she reminded Jack of Rosalind Russell in the movie *Auntie Mame*.

Overheard from the adjacent table, the wife was saying, "You know, if you can't find any locals to dance with, I'm usually available."

"Oooops! Guess I'm on the shit list, huh?"

"You'd better believe it, Roscoe. I'm for dragging my ass outta here and heading home. You're about as much fun to be around as a one-legged tap dancer."

Soon they finished their drinks and left.

Ruby wanted to know when Jack would be returning to the digs. She missed Doc. She felt abandoned.

"Probably tomorrow."

"I haven't seen that horrible man for almost two weeks and I need to hear his voice; to argue with him; to hold him. Oh, hell! I'm probably in love with the fool!"

"Nothing wrong with that, Ruby. Happens to the best of us."

Agnes smiled openly.

"Anyhow, he needs to be taken down a peg or two. Acts like he's too good to mingle with the rest of us."

"I'll set that straight, you betcha! He'll be gentle as a lamb when *I* get done with him."

CHAPTER THIRTY-SIX

When Jack returned to the digs, Timco was busy erecting an oven out of river rock. Slabs of sandstone were being used as shelf spaces for uncooked batter and finished product.

"Looks pretty good, Timco. What are you going to use it for?"

"What else? Sourdough, of course! I got me some starter and plan on baking up a storm. I love sourdough bread!"

"You never cease to amaze me, old friend. Is there anything you're not able to do?"

"To tell the truth, I can't chew bubble gum and walk at the same time."

"I can understand that. You're quite spastic most of the time. See ya later."

*   *   *

The workers on the mound to the east were progressing at a good pace. The earth was fairly soft, with few rocks to impede them.

Harry kept glancing over at Celeste. She seemed to be tiring.

"Don't you think you'd better rest for awhile, Cheri? It's quite hot and you haven't taken a break for a long time."

"Don't torment me, Harry. You persist on saying the work's too hard on me. I'm enjoying it, so leave me alone!"

"You should breathe through your nose, dear, it helps to prevent dehydration."

He was rewarded with, "Humph!"

He had learned early in their marriage that she had spunk. When she was in one of her moods it was best to stay clear.

Timco called for someone to bring him a sieve. He uncovered several shards and wished to screen the next few shovelfuls to inspect them for pieces.

The result was the discovery of traces of charcoal.

He called a temporary halt to the digging.

"I'll show this stuff to Doc and see what he's got to say. Take a break everyone."

*   *   *

After two weeks on site, Three Bears was becoming a recognizable fixture. The old man was adept at legerdemain and could captivate young and old alike.

He wasn't merely indulged by Dragonfly, he was venerated as an entertainer and for his prophetic statements. She would often invite him into her Hogan in the evening for a meal and a pipe and they would enjoy smoke talk.

If one of the workmen came down with an ill, Three Bears would sing, a capella, what appeared to be a dirge in a strange tongue and the person would magically be cured.

It was amazing!

One day he was near the east mound observing the diggings. There was a small flock of feral goats grazing contentedly on the rise; defecating at will—on, and around the mound.

"They're masticators of everything that grows above ground," he said disgustingly as he tried shooing them away. He finally had to throw some good-sized rocks in their direction to get them moving.

He asked Timco if they were making any progress.

"I figure we'll find out what this is before long, with a little luck."

Three Bears scowled at this remark. "Good luck has the scent of perspiration around it. It doesn't come easy, friend."

"You're probably right, old man. The shovels will lead the way, eh?"

He took a break then and headed down to the kitchen area for a cup of joe. As he passed Ruth Golden Eagle's team, he heard one of the men whistling.

Another numb skull [he thought]. He grunted in disgust.

The man hefted a heavy bucket filled with earth and continued his whistling, not missing a beat.

Timco stopped and confronted him.

"I was told by my Top that only fools and bosun's mates whistle. You don't appear to be in the Navy, so I assume you're in the other category. Besides, it brings bad luck, so knock it off and give more energy to the work."

CHAPTER THIRTY-SEVEN

They were sitting on camp stools around a small fire, hankering for a bit of heat to ward off the early morning chill, chatting and enjoying some of Timco's baked goods; coffee mugs cradled in their hands.

There was just enough smoke to keep the mosquitoes at bay; enough light to wake the birds who were chirping loudly.

Sounds at sunrise and sunset carry. When the warm morning air slides over the cold air of night, sound carries better than at other times. It has to do with the density of the two kinds of air. Sound travels farther in dense, cold air.

Birds want their songs to carry as far as possible, so that their many rivals will be aware that the territory is occupied.

Harry was the first to break the pregnant silence.

"As usual, it's been more than educational, Jack. But the gist of the matter is, we've stayed longer than planned and should be getting back home."

Celeste nodded her agreement and smiled weakly.

Jack peered into the dwindling flames.

"I've probably ignored you two more than I wanted to, but this project is getting under my skin and I'd hate to say I left when it was half finished."

"I have the same feelings, Jack," Celeste said. "I really enjoyed sweating over a shovel, hoping to find something interesting. Something I could brag about back home. It didn't happen, but it was nice daydreaming about the—what if?"

"Same with me, mon amie," Harry added. "Besides, I think I've given officer Cooper enough information for him to close the case. He's one fine man."

"I have to agree with you there," Jack said.

"Just on the QT, Jack, he said there was one of his DEA buddies snooping around and he's come up with some interesting facts."

"Yeh, I know. Ran into him in town. He's got to be a city dude and hasn't the foggiest on how to blend in."

There was a deafening scream over by the north wall.

"What the—?" Jack started to ask.

"Now what?" Doc asked no one in particular.

"Edur fell into the trench. He looks hurt bad."

Doc raised both hands in exasperation. "Someone give him a hand. Get him out of there!"

"He only fell about eight feet, but he must have scraped his knee on something. It's bleeding fiercely," a voice in the background said.

"Take wounded knee over to see if Three Bears, the soothsayer, can do something for him, Doc ordered. "He might be able to remove the hex on him or something like that. Then again, you might have Dragonfly kiss it to make it well. I need him back on the job immediately, if not sooner. We're falling behind schedule I keep telling you all."

Jack assisted Edur over to Three Bear's tent.

"Can you do anything for this wounded person?"

"Set him down here on the wolf pelts."

He began to chant, accompanied by a gourd rattle. The *chantways* focus on curing and can be performed according to one of three rituals. He was using the *Lifeway Chant ('Iináájí)* used to treat injuries caused by accidents.

Dragonfly came into the tent, a mean look about her.

"Will you stop with that mumbling and gourd rattling? Hold him down long enough for me to dab some of this ointment on him."

Edur had a wild look in his eyes as the two old Indians ministered to him.

"What are these two old, crazy Indians trying to do to me? [he wondered].

"What's that you're using, Dragonfly?" Jack asked. "Looks like Unguentine my mother used on me. Same kind of green can."

"It's my own remedy. Got aloe and some other roots and herbs in a pine-pitch base. Good stuff and it works wonders."

"Well, Three Bears, I'd say you're an absolute farce! Dragonfly's stuff seems to be doing the trick." Jack chided. "Edur quieted down real nice."

"Why so, a farce? I don't promise any more than your weirdly dressed priests who hold communion with their vile wine and cardboard wafers. You Irish have your leprechauns—the Hawaiians have their menehunes—the Persians have their jinnies. Whose to say my chants to the *dighin diné*—*Holy People*—are any less revered or accepted?"

"Who gave you the idea you were a genuine medicine man anyhow?"

Three Bears cordial reply was, "Mind your own damned business!"

Shamans were a figure, idiosyncratic, not answerable to any synod, of which the Catholic church represented. They were an irritating challenge to the missionaries and teachings of the priests.

"I never claimed to be a shaman. It was thrust upon me by the native people who regarded me as their channel to the spirits. I was their healer," Three Bears mentioned. "I was nominated, you might say, and I began to firmly believe I could accomplish the miracles they wanted."

"Didn't you feel like you were pulling wool over their eyes?"

"Not really. I could preach that alcohol was an evil spirit or demon and those who were captured in it's talons would nod and agree, but then head out for another bottle. They knew, deep down, how bad it was but continued to use it as a crutch. I finally got tired of preaching this moral negative and moved on to other, tangible, non-ghostly things that were more understandable. This, they expected."

Jack couldn't think of anything to say. He merely shrugged.

Three Bears filled in the silence.

"What don't you like about the shamans? They're really no different than the priests of your religion, who also claim to be healers."

"It's hard to say. They both claim to answer to a higher authority only they wear different clothes."

"There you have it!" Three Bears exclaimed. He had nothing more to say. A tear formed in his eye just before he turned away.

Of course, Jack wasn't privy to the functions of *medicine elders* as they were called, to secure the help of the spirit world for the benefit of all. Sometimes they might seek help in healing a disease, sometimes for healing the psyche, sometimes to promote harmony between humans and nature.

In order to function as a bridge between the natural and spiritual world, the person must be validated. Most medicine men and women, study through a society, such as the Navajo Blessingway or apprentice themselves to a teacher for twenty to thirty years—or both. They take themselves seriously.

Some people consider them *Witch Doctors*. This is technically inaccurate. Shamans perform a plethora of functions, among which is healing, storytelling and songs. First Nations peoples often seek communion with spirits through a vision quest performed by their shaman.

As the Catholic influence spread with Spanish colonization, a definite denouncing of shamanism occurred, calling it devil worshipping and shamans were put to death, not so much for preaching their so-called evils, but because the Spanish priests couldn't cope with not having absolute control over the indigenous peoples.

The *Hatalii* performed more interesting ceremonies.

Jack's understanding of the Catholic priesthood was a rather vague recollection of teachings by his childhood priest. He was aware that a cleric's education lasts between five and six years, depending on the Program of Priestly Foundation, after successfully completing a four-year university degree, followed by an additional four to five years of seminary education.

Too much time studying to suit him.

These strict tenets were what made him decide to go into the marble business. He couldn't see being strapped down by the church. Anyhow, his voice was changing and he was asked to leave the choir— an enjoyable time in his youth.

As he walked way from Three Bears he noticed a group of kids kneeling in the soil, engrossed in the antics of a dung beetle. This one was a roller, who would roll a wad of dung into a ball and deposit it into a brooding chamber as a future food source.

Most dung beetles search for food with the aid of their strong sense of smell. Once they've located a source, they roll the ball, following a straight line, towards their final destination. They move rapidly in order to keep it away from other beetles who might attempt to steal it.

Dung beetles play an important role in agriculture as well as helping to clean up an area. By burying and consuming dung, they improve the soil structure, much like a fishing worm will do. They also protect livestock by removing the dung that invites pests, such as flies, that tend to carry disease.

CHAPTER THIRTY-EIGHT

Here comes a bundle of trouble, Yellow Fox surmised. It was big Billy Stillwell, all puffed up and ready for battle.

"What's the problem, Billy?"

"It's them damned uneducated savages! We got the barracks all ready and most of the old people won't move in. they say too many corners for spirits to hide in. They want to stay in their round-bottomed tipis and tents.!"

"Don't sweat it, Billy. There's plenty of the younger ones that will make it a temp home. I'll talk to Three Bears and see if he can calm them down."

"Okay, but me and the guys who put that thing up are highly pissed-off. We busted our cans getting it ready so soon and then the idiots won't even come inside to take a look!"

"Right. Just another day on the job, Billy. You think *you* got problems, go talk to Doc for awhile."

"Aw, hell! What's next on your job list?"

Doc sat on a stool at his workbench in the Quonset. Several small piles of dirt were before him. Some were laced with bits of charcoal, others had minute pieces of potshards. He was very excited.

Jack strolled in, and noticing Doc's glee, asked what all the fuss was about.

"I think we've discovered part of a civilization. Samples of charcoal were found in these piles of dirt, possibly indicating we're digging over an ancient kiln. The other amazing find is these pieces of shards. I realize this stuff is very small, but we have the possibility of unearthing much more."

"You mean that if we uncover a kiln at that mound there's a good chance the rest of this area will be like a museum of treasure?"

"Exactly. The type of kiln we uncover will tell us a lot about the inhabitants. Of course, I can't relate a kiln to a pueblo. Different cultures. This is all very interesting and I'll have to contact the authorities to get someone out here to verify our finds."

"You mean there's different kinds of kilns?"

"Oh, yes. You've got wood-drying kilns, ceramic kilns, charcoal making kilns, cremation kilns—."

"I get the picture. So we need to uncover most of it to see what kind we have here, right? I'll get the crew working a little harder so that when your expert shows up we'll have something to show him—or her."

*   *   *

Nearing the site in a cloud of trailing dust was a relic from the junkyard.

A horn blared announcing the arrival.

It was a sickly-green Studebaker pickup, canted slightly to the driver's side. It was surely a sad-looking conveyance.

Ole Oleson didn't have a horse that could carry his mass for any length of time, and as a result, he used the truck for round-ups. Range cattle hooked it with a passion but it managed to survive the batterings.

It pulled up with a screech of brakes. Ole, along with Frenchy Burgoyne, climbed out and surveyed the area casually.

"Whatcha doin' out here, Ole?" Timco asked.

"Heard through the grapevine you was needin' more hands, so me and Frenchy here, decided to take off a few days and pitch in. Okay?"

"Sure. The more the merrier."

"Where do you want us?"

"Over there by that mound," he indicated with an outstretched arm. "Doc wants to get most of whatever's underneath uncovered so he can find out what we've got. You'll find extra shovels leaning against the Quonset."

"Okay. We're on it."

Ole took off with a slight hitch in one leg.

"You okay, Ole?"

"Yep. Might be a bit gimpy, but I can handle a shovel, you betcha! Come on, skinny one, we've got work to do!"

CHAPTER THIRTY-NINE

Coruscating colors were streaking across the western sky—similar to the aurora borealis.

Suddenly the sky darkened. A continuous cannonade of thunder, interspersed with stabbing, sharp fingers of lightning filled the air. In the intervals of the war in the firmament, yells of terror were heard from the workers. Wind gusts of seventy-miles-per-hour were grabbing at everything not tied down. Flying sand and debris limited visibility to less than ten feet.

The face of the encampment was being altered and deformed. The wind disturbed large amounts of earth and sand and deposited it at it's whim in convenient locations.

The sun was obliterated. It was very dark. Rain was now spitting from the menacing clouds.

People ran helter-skelter seeking shelter. Soon the barracks and Quonset hut were filled with humanity. Exhausted from fighting the tempest, they huddled together like wind-blown crows. They all realized it was of no use to defy nature. It was simply a matter of keeping the dust and sand from invading nostrils and lungs.

Out of compassion, and of necessity, meager meals were doled out in an attempt to appease the throng which consisted of almost seventy people now, considering the additional newcomers that were added to the initial group of Indians.

The temperature dropped considerably and Franklin stoves in both buildings were lit off, alleviating some of the anxiety.

"The storm is about a mile away," Yellow Fox announced between claps of thunder.

"How can you tell that?" someone asked.

"Count the time between the lightning flash and the thunder clap. Every five seconds equals one mile."

"Geez, Yellow Fox is there anything you don't know something about?"

"Probably, but I haven't run across it yet."

It was calm for a short while and then the wind, remembering it's purpose, blew once more in gusts up to 45 miles per hour. This situation lasted for another three hours.

Finally, the tempest abated. Movement was seen outside the buildings as the captured people ventured once more to their work stations.

To Doc's dismay, several feet of earth and sand had been removed from around the north wall. The base was now visible. He had his helpers dig in the area, using caution.

His shovel uncovered a small cache of strange-looking items made of lignum vitae. Idols of some sort. The material wasn't native to this part of the world. The carved items could possibly be of Aztec origin. His heart took on arrhythmia.

It would be determined later by radiocarbon assay they were of an age of 5,000 years, plus or minus.

He took a momentous vertical leap of joy—at least three inches. After all, he was nearing forty-five and any further exertion could prove fatal to his out of shape body.

He looked up from his stance with a strange, crooked smile on his face, a dampness around his eyes.

"We've done it!" he announced proudly. "By God, we've done it!"

There was now the impetus to continue with the project.

He slumped down, head between his knees, and wept openly. It was his greatest triumph since he helped with the Mayan excavations at Yaxhá in Guatemala. He clambered out of the trench, yelling loudly, "Everyone! Stop whatever you're doing! We need to be very careful while digging now. Take a break until we can figure out our next move."

Three Fingers came up to Yellow Fox. In his guttural language he was directing him to meet with his grandfather. Yellow Fox had an epistemological attitude regarding the Navajo tongue. It was becoming increasingly harder to converse or understand most of the dialects.

In precise English he told the youngster to take a long breath while he made up his mind whether to obey the ancient one.

He field-stripped his cigarette, decapitating the glowing red end with a flick of his finger and scattered the tobacco; then wet his fingers and rolled the paper into a small ball, dropped it to the ground, and mashed it beneath his boot.

Marine training. Old habits die hard.

CHAPTER FORTY

The three men were relaxing in the cantina, waiting for a reply to Doc's telephone call to the museum curator.

"Seem's to me the town's mighty empty of men folks," Timco observed.

"Now that you mention it, you're right. It's damned spooky," Jack replied.

They motioned for Han Po. "What's going on?"

"Bu` kan sh éxiang!—dreadful consequences are in the making. It seems the men formed a posse comitatus and are searching for that evil man who calls himself a priest. The one who deserted the children during the fire. Cooper, that giant of an Indian policeman, has taken off to detain them, if possible."

"Does that mean you're the only man left in town?" Doc asked.

"That is probably true. I'm not a person who takes pleasure in chasing criminals. I also have concerns that my business would be invaded if left unattended," he answered with downcast eyes.

"That's the smartest thing to do, Han Po. Those idiots chasing around out there with loaded guns could get into a heap of trouble if shooting starts," Timco advised.

*   *   *

Cooper overtook the mob and convinced them to return to town. He would continue the search alone.

He was no longer searching for a so-called priest. The investigators working the case came up with some interesting facts.

It seems that one Dylan Moriarity, an escapee from Joliet prison, was now in the area posing as a Catholic priest. His cohort, one Renaldo Dominquez, originally from Oaxaca, Mexico, was now missing. He was a known trafficker in drugs.

Hiding out in the church was a conundrum of Moriarity's existence. It appears he walked out of the prison dispensary just as slick as you please wearing a lab coat, during an altercation and fire in the cell block that held the attention of the guards. He's considered armed, dangerous and cunning.

* * *

Moriarity rode a sorrel mare, about three years old. It seemed to have stamina for a long ride. He made no effort to conceal his tracks. He'd been on the trail for three days now and hadn't had any sleep, to speak of. He finally took a break and slept for an hour or so beneath a piñon pine.

Nerves, or the simmering fever he developed from too much exposure to the elements, woke him. His eyes seemed to have sunk into his head, leaving in their place two blurred dark holes. He smelled bad.

He sat on the sorrel in the middle of a small creek that was rushing and overflowing it's banks due to recent rains further up in the mountains. He eased the reins and the horse dipped it's head and drank thirstily.

He finally decided that he was free and clear and rested the night beside a scant fire—just enough to ward off the chill.

The next day he came upon an old line shack with a stone chimney from which the mortar was crumbling. Half the sod roof was missing. The other half was propped up with several corral railings. Two rattlers, seeking a warm spot, joined him, and curled up in feed sacks in the corner.

Cooper approached the soddy cautiously. He flattened against the front and strained to hear the slightest sound. He leaped in front of the door and kicked it in. Some huge thing hurtled towards his face. He fired twice. It was a large owl that almost knocked his hat off.

Moriarity was gone.

In the morning Cooper shot a rabbit and gorged himself on the roasted meat, packing some away that he would eat before it spoiled.

Moriarity dropped out of the saddle and left the reins lying across the withers, a concerned look on his face. The horse was limping and acted like it had a strained leg. Being a concrete type, he didn't have the slightest idea what to do about it. A cursory examination would have revealed a pebble caught in one it's hooves. He was ignorant of such action.

Now it was a matter of hiking it if he were to outdistance his pursuer. He staggered along, ever conscious of his possible capture, contemplating ways to overwhelm him when he made an appearance.

He had all to venture and nothing to lose. He was determined that his last effort in iniquity should be worthy of his cleverness.

Creosote, mesquite and various other nasty chapparal bushes tore at this clothing. There wasn't a bush big enough to shelter a horned toad. A roadrunner streaked across his path, seeking a morsel.

This crappy country would drive a dog insane looking for a place to raise a leg.

Every now and then he paused and listened, but as yet heard nothing. He was running out of energy rapidly. He desperately needed water.

At each agonizing step the ground became rockier. Here and there were small dry washes which he was obliged to crawl up and down the sides on his hands and knees. Not especially to his liking.

Cooper was gaining steadily on the wandering criminal. He rode across a rincon to an outcropping of gypsum—produced when sea water evaporated during pre-Permian times. The pasterns of his horse were covered with talcum-like dust.

And then, he espied the staggering Moriarity. He fired a shot in the air to warn him. Moriarity continued on a few more paces, undaunted, and then collapsed face down in the brush. He was done for. His limbs trembled; his lips were parched and half-open in an expression of agony.

He offered no resistance when Cooper lashed his arms behind him and placed a loop of a lariat around his neck.

"You'll enjoy the long walk back to town, mister shit-head. I should shoot you now, and save the State an expensive trial, but you might enjoy that too much.

"Now git!"

The strain from the lariat on his pommel was becoming more pronounced. Moriarity was barely keeping up with the horse. He'd been fed a few morsels of jerky, washed down with a sip of tepid water. Cooper was fain to allow that much nourishment, but he needed to bring the culprit in alive.

They came upon a small herd of free-roaming feral horses—mustangs—and he decided it would speed up their travels if he captured one. The mustangs were descended from Iberian stock brought over to this country by the Spaniards in the 1600's.

He hog-tied Moriarity, left him propped against a boulder, and proceeded to rope one of the frisky animals. As expected, it was quite ornery and refused to take a halter. He finally grabbed an ear and forced it to the ground. He cinched it's head to a foreleg and left it lying there for some considerable time until it calmed down.

It was an unhappy animal.

Cutting a length from his lariat, he produced a hackamore by which Moriarity could control the beast. He warned him, however, to be gentle using it as it could cause severe pain and swelling of the nose otherwise. A distraught horse can become mighty mean.

With a boost on the rump he managed to get his prisoner up on the horse. He ran a cinch from each of his legs under the horse's belly. This would prevent a quick escape. Riding bareback might also squelch any thoughts of running off seem unlikely. It gave Cooper a certain amount of enjoyment when Moriarity complained that his legs and rump were being rubbed raw.

They were now making fairly good time and were about four days out from town.

CHAPTER FORTY-ONE

It was a beautiful, clear Sunday morning. Jack and Agnes were sitting on the bench outside the café waiting for it to open. Aromas from Mindy's cooking were exciting their saliva glands. The air had a pinch of frost as a cold wind began blowing in from the far-off mountains. The first colors of autumn were glowing on the few trees in town.

Summer was gasping for breath.

She turned slightly toward him and asked what he thought of her new dress.

"That's a dress? It's hardly big enough to make a good snot rag."

"Thanks a ton, Jack. I thought you might like it— just a little anyhow."

"Well, it does sort of show me enough to get riled up."

She grimaced.

Suddenly there was a sound.

Unheard in town for over two-hundred years.

The knell of the church bell! Jack felt the reverberations move through him. It would be his gift to the memory of Ruth. The bell rang once more with tremulous vibrations as if it's teeth were chattering.

The sound sent some residents scurrying for a hiding place. Some reached for pistols and rifles. Others were jolted to grab their horses, quickly saddle up, and head out of town.

Ever since that first Sunday at the Estancia, Jack was determined to purchase a bell for the old church.

It needed a bell.

He had Cliff buy it secretly, and with two of his workers, they installed it unobserved. Jack wished to remain an unknown benefactor, to remain anonymous.

A tear filled the corner of an eye, when the first sounds filled the air. He was standing still now, a strange expression on his face.

Agnes became concerned. She had never seen him like this before.

"Is there something wrong, Jack? Can I do anything for you?"

"I'm just fine. Never felt better," he answered with a wink. "Let's get something to eat. I'm starved!"

*   *   *

Timco noticed a newcomer in camp. He was lanky, had a pox-marked face and looked rugged.

"Who are you and how'd you get here?" he demanded, fist clenched.

"Name's Hotar. I'm relative to the sidewinders."

"Of course you are."

"The wind chased me here. Looks like you could use a bit more help."

"You got that right."

"Who's the honcho? I'll make him an offer."

"It's Doc, and he's in the hut. Better hobble your horse away from the rest. Looks like it's having a fit."

"Nothing to worry about. Got into some loco weed aways back. Be right as rain shortly."

*   *   *

Activity at the digs was picking up. One of Cliff's flatbed trucks arrived with Hotar, the sidewinder, riding shotgun. On the bed was a small

BobCat. Hotar proclaimed that now they could move some major dirt and get to the bottom of things.

Two other arrivals were now on site. One was Doctor Z. L. Helene Piquette, a paleontologist from San Juan College. Dr. Piquette and Doc Cambresis were seated on stools at the work bench in the Quonset. They had their heads together discussing the lignum vitae find, charcoal specks and some bone fragments uncovered so far.

She was very excited. Her cheeks were pink and her eyes glowed brightly. Doc really admired this woman; breeding, intelligence and enthusiasm; things important in his own life, she had in abundance, plus youth and a rare beauty.

She noted that lignum vitae wasn't native growth in this area and that the idol seemed to be of Aztec origin. Doc merely raised an eyebrow at this statement, having decided those redundant facts for himself.

The pottery shards were another matter. Until larger pieces were uncovered, they would remain a mystery. The bone fragments would be sent to her lab.

A man named Justine, from the museum, was the other newcomer in camp. He left a small shadow, and carried a little notebook in which to record and verify all finds.

The pages were all blank.

He wandered aimlessly for an hour or so; exasperated. He was of small stature with sallow skin and dark eyes which seemed to drain the color from the rest of his face. Eventually he drove into town to mingle with the locals at the cantina. He acted in a foofarraw manner by purchasing an outlandish western-style shirt from Don at the mercantile to replace his white business one, figuring it might make him blend in.

It didn't work.

The shirt made him stand out like a gypsy.

*   *   *

Hotar, the sidewinder, riding the BobCat, was busy uncovering layers of silt and earth from around the kiln area. He worked with exuberance and expertise. He seemed to be everywhere at once and was moving an enormous amount of overburden.

Billy Stillwell, the large Indian, was wielding a pickaxe with the ease of a toy, a fierce scowl on his face. His group had joined Ruth Golden Eagle's and he was determined to outdo that damned machine! His pectorals were becoming breast-like from the exertion.

The equipment on this site consisted of eight wheelbarrows, six pickaxes, seven shovels, a few buckets and many woven baskets.

The men with the pickaxes were working on a fifteen-foot wide section of trench where the kiva was supposedly located.

Shovelers loaded the softened earth into the buckets and baskets which were then carried to a sifting area. Once inspected, the residue was then carried to a deep ravine for disposal.

The accumulated dirt was transposing the landscape into a flat plain.

Mike entered the Quonset and excused himself for butting in.

"Sorry, Doc, didn't mean to bother you, but we've run into a door at the north wall and I thought you might want to check it out."

"You bet! I'll be right along."

He swiveled on his stool to face Dr. Piquette.

"If you don't mind, I'll run over there to see what they've found."

"Go right ahead. I caught a whiff of coffee brewing. I'll grab some and take a breather."

"Right. Be back in a wink."

When he wasn't tending the kitchen, Endur was at the digs working with his twin.

"That wheelbarrow's only half full, Andoni."

"So's your skull."

"Keep if up and I'll thump you alongside that thick gourd of yours with a shovel."

"Bet me!" Andoni responded and pushed off with his half load, humming.

*   *   *

The elders were gathered in Dragonfly's Hogan discussing progress on the digs and other matters of importance. Three Bears now held them in sway.

He cleared his throat and began.

"I came to know the ways of the shamans. What people wanted to hear. I would do ceremonies for different illnesses. Some worked, others failed. I had a small pouch with healing items: turquoise, abalone shell, red coral stone, eagle feathers, pollen, flint blades and obsidian.

I had another pouch made of deerskin with white clay, red ocher, crystal, opal, jasper, snakewood, cigarettes rolled in oak leaves, plants with medicinal effect, natural antibiotics, herbs that constricted blood vessels and reduce bleeding, and others. All these items were part of a healing ceremony, taught to me by an ancient shaman.

"I will be disgraced if I lie to you—so I must speak the truth, hunh?

"I tired of preaching moral negatives and moved on to other tangible non-ghostly things. More understandable and life-giving. The people expected it.

"It was all part of a ritual. Just like in the church. They have hymns, incense, candles, icons and such.

"We hold sacred dances. The church holds it's processions with bells and smoke."

One of the old men rolled onto his stomach, hugging himself, and laughing hysterically. Then the reason for all this activity reached the others. It was a vicious fart that was to be the destiny of the meeting. A green sour-smelling fog surrounded the old man's head. It appeared feeble-looking—almost like ectoplasm.

"Really!" was all Dragonfly could manage between futile gasps for breath.

Several of the elders sprang up and departed the Hogan in haste, choking for air. Their kinnikinick stoked pipes were dropped unceremoniously; left lying in the dust.

"I reckon the meeting is over," Three Bears said, straight-faced.

*   *   *

Doc wandered his demesne in a stupor. The architecture of this edifice followed no particular scheme. He assumed the pueblo was erected in the normal configuration. Why is this particular door facing north, towards the cliff face? [he wondered].

At the other end of the trench Mike encountered an overburden of course mica sand, beneath which were found shells and endoskeletons of strange, small animals. He motioned for Doc to come have a look-see.

"I'm assuming this area was a reef in the sea many eons ago. I'll get Dr. Piquette over here to verify what you've found."

"The findings here are extraordinary," she said, upon examination. "I'll take a few samples back to my lab and run a test on them."

Mike resumed his probing. Back along the trench the remains of another wall was located. It was becoming obvious this area wasn't over a kiva.

Two days later the remains of a large room were uncovered. In an alcove of one wall a complete skeleton was found.

Mike, Timco and the two doctor/scientists began carefully to expose the bones with small trowels and brushes, careful not to disturb anything else. Dr. Piquette examined the skull, and with a strange look, mentioned casually, "Genetically this skull isn't of Athabaskan ancestry, rather it appears to be Semitic."

She brushed away a bit more residue. "It's abundantly clear. See the high cheekbones and elongated face.? Also, this person was much too tall to be an Indian of many years ago. They were generally of much smaller stature—about five feet one or two inches."

She took a measurement of the humerus bone and found it to be fifteen inches long, making this person over six feet tall; using the five-to-one ratio of determining height in a human.

Doc added a bit of information. "Notice he's grasping a caul in his hand. He was most likely very superstitious. According to legend, it's supposed to bring good luck to the believer, but obviously it did no good for this person."

"After I've gone over the entire skeleton, there's no indication that he was killed by trauma," Piquette said. "I'm inclined to think his death was caused by some undetermined vector."

"Never-the-less, this is an incredible find, don't you agree?" Doc asked her.

"It certainly is," she answered with a wide grin.

Edur, helping Mike, began jumping around like a bead of water in a hot skillet.

"What's with that idiot now?" Timco asked.

"The dumb ass only stubbed his toe. He's a disaster waiting for a place to happen, that's for sure."

"Well, Cambrensis, I think I may now say Q.E.D. and congratulate you on an exciting discovery. You realize, of course, that archaeology is considered a luxury science. It takes considerable funding to sustain a project."

"That's more or less true. There's always been an ambivalent relationship between anthropology and archaeology. After all, archaeology is the potshards science of someone else's rubbish."

"Well put, Doctor. Now, I'd like to pack up some specimens and get into town. I have a small amount of lab equipment with me, but it's best I take them to the college. This has been truly a wonder—amazing to say the least."

"That's a fine idea. I'll shut down the digs temporarily. Several of us will accompany you into town and take a much needed break."

Hauling a water trailer—the word *Potable* painted on it's sides—two chemical outhouses, several crates of commodity items, and Mike, Cliff swung into the site amid cheers and waves.

Everyone was ready to partially abandon the self-imposed water rationing. It would still be chancy, but at least they wouldn't have to rely wholly on boiled water from the river.

Mike was greeted in a like manner. Since his encounter with the rash, and a fairly long absence from the site, people wondered if he had survived.

He now sported a black eye patch over his left eye socket, giving him the appearance of a Caribbean pirate. It made him look quite debonair. The children loved it!

Of course, the word *Potable* raised many eyebrows and caused consternation among several Indians. They figured it was another white man's way of demeaning them for lack of a proper education.

Chapter Forty-Two

When Celeste spotted the water trailer pulling in, she was ecstatic
"Now I can at least cleanse myself in a half-civilized toilet.
It's been more than a week and I'm feeling sooo grimy."
She didn't think it very wise to ride over to the river for a dip—alone. There were most likely cotton mouth water moccasins or other nasty things waiting to pounce on her there.
She had Timco rig up a large wash tub behind the water trailer, with a privacy curtain of canvas, so she could at least wet down her whole body, away from prying eyes.
It was pure heaven!

One of the Indian girls was a bit foppish, but a good, steady worker. She was constantly uttering inanities such as, "How utterly utter," or "It's simply too, too." She also managed to be around Harry as often as possible.
Celeste considered her to be seductively beautiful but a promiscuous young woman. A study in jealousy and self-torment. A truly amoral person who vacillates between guilt and moral smugness.
She is a splendidly endowed creature, whose feline strength and beauty exert animal-like magnetism. Her complexion, a dark golden ochre, was suffused with the rose-colored cheeks of robust health.

When it was time for a break she would sidle up to Harry and linger a bit too long for Celeste's liking.

She would explain why she hung around longer than was necessary. "I have the slow digestion of a snake. It takes me longer to eat," she would announce coyly.

One day she approached Celeste, hands covering her breasts. "I reckon mine will match up to yours, close enough," she bragged.

"Maybe so, but the rest of your body needs some looking into. Especially that mouth of yours."

After a few days of these outwardly brazen displays, Celeste finally told Harry to stay away from the vixen; ignore her as much as possible.

He finally had to tell the young woman to leave him alone. "Don't you realize that's my wife standing over there, ready to do you in?"

She had been rebuked.

It would be shameful if she cried—if she showed the least signs of emotion. It wasn't the way of her people.

To save face, she asked Yellow Fox to assign her to another group.

*   *   *

Dragonfly had the ear of the young man firmly in her grasp. She led him forcibly to Yellow Fox, the negotiator.

"This one has been caught stealing from his fellow man. He was seen entering two tents and leaving with pilfered goods."

"Leave him with me."

"What am I going to do with you, young man? This isn't good."

"Do with me? Who do you think you are, the Big Chief?"

"Nope. Just the head cheese in this operation. You'll take orders from no one but me, got it?"

Yellow Fox's eyes bespoke power; deep and glistening with intelligence. His eyes normally appeared kind and cautious, a hint of humor behind them.

"You sound like some friggin' jar-head, and with that haircut and all."

"Watch your tongue, boot! There's women around. Anyhow, that's fine with me—the original Marine."

"But you see, Mr. Navajo Marine, you're from but a minor tribe to the Apache and Hopi. *I'm* a proud Jicarilla. I'm called John Manuelito (an English name he considered a sobriquet) or *Mai-déc-Kiz-ne.* Wolf Neck, to you, and I'm from Stinking Lake on the rez. So what?"

"Of course, you are. Let me explain something to you, Wolf Neck."

He scrupled as the young man turned his head away slightly, ignoring him.

"Oh, fuggetit—."

These young people of the new generation couldn't give a rat's ass less.

Yellow Fox was painfully aware of his own heritage, especially the Indian half, and wasn't all too proud of it. The Norwegian half wasn't a helluva lot better.

Apparently, according to the Book of Mormon, white men came from ancient Israel in 600 B.C., reaching the New World by boat. Some descendents, the Lamanites, decided not to obey the laws laid down by their brethren, the Nephites—who were supposedly good— and waged a thousand-year war against them.

The Lamanites won the long war but were stamped with dark skin as a sign of their evil doings.

Those of the dark skin were eventually classified as Indians, or the fallen souls. They could, however, be redeemed by sincere Mormon missionaries if they ceased their wanton ways. The proselytizing failed and the Indians returned to their old ways and were thoroughly chastised by the church.

Yellow Fox knew of the *milk before meat* teachings and regarded them with a somewhat jaundiced eye.

Yellow Fox studied the tall, faintly menacing young Indian who stood before him now in stoical silence. His release from the project was inevitable and it didn't make things easier that he genuinely admired the youth. His eyes scanned him but didn't register remorse.

The truth is more obvious than the sun.

He obeyed instructions faithfully. He was always one of the first on the job in the morning. He was generous with his purloined smokes. Notwithstanding all those attributes, he was, never-the-less, a kleptomanic. This can't be tolerated.

Theft was a choice. Also the vice of sloth. Many thieves believed it was easier to steal than to work for what they wanted.

This young man would need to be chastised for his repugnant behavior.

Another embarrassed youth was led to the confrontation. He was Storm Cloud, brother of the culprit.

"I should kill you for what you've done!" he yelled. "Our family won't be able to show their faces in public!"

"You must realize, Storm Cloud, that fratricide is considered an unnatural crime amongst the tribes," Timco explained. "I know you must be very mad at your brother, but that's no solution. What I will impose will be far worse, in the long run. He shall be exiled. He won't be exculpated for his crimes. There will be no solatium—compensation for being kicked out of the tribe. He will forever have a black mark against his name on the rez. It is considered a very strong sentence."

Dragonfly nodded in agreement. "You have done well, Yellow Fox. The others will respect your decision."

CHAPTER FORTY-THREE

Three Bears, the venerable story teller, called Yellow Fox to his small part of the world.

They sat cross-legged, facing each other, across a small fire fed with cedar chips. The aromatic smoke spiraled upward, finally dissipating into the quiet evening air.

"Why do you insist on calling me *Sikyaatayo,* Three Bears?"

"Mostly because I like the sound of it. When Three Fingers and myself stayed for a short time in Oraibi, on the Third Mesa, I learned the Hopi called themselves *Hopituh Shi-nu-mu,* The Peaceful People. I liked the fact they have respect for all things," he added, after passing the calabash over. "Your name, Yellow Fox, is *Sikyaatayo* in Hopi and it fits you well."

"I suppose it's not so bad having two Indian names," Yellow Fox surmised. "They call me **T**iso maiittsooi in the Navajo tongue. I prefer either one to my given name, Cameron."

Three Bears squinted across the smoke. "I have noticed, Yellow Fox, that every time that Chinaman, Han Po, blurts out one of his idioms, you get excited and seem to understand the gibberish."

"Yes. It's strange, indeed. I can't explain it, but Chinese comes easy for me. Some of the Navajo old ones are also able to understand the language. I hear there's DNA evidence that the Navajo are related in some way to the Chinese. I don't argue the point."

"That's very interesting—if true. Tell me a little of your background. You seem to be a very interesting person."

Yellow Fox eased back on his elbows.

"I learned from my grandfather, on my mother's side, that all Army officers were college or West Point graduates, but not necessarily good leaders. While he was on the Long Walk it was usually the non-coms who kept order and maintained discipline.

"Even though he was a minor chief of the Tewa tribe, he was required to walk among the people as a common criminal. This was all whilst facing the opprobrium of the soldiers as he defended the right of his status as a chief."

Three Bears took a long drag on the pipe, letting the smoke escape slowly. He then passed it across to Yellow Fox.

"That's a most interesting tale. I too, had relatives in the Long Walk. It was Kit Carson and his troops that were told to raid the land, destroying everything, including the crops, in hopes of getting the Navajo to surrender. That Long Walk you speak of was a total disaster. After five years at Fort Sumner a treaty was signed and my relatives joined in for the reverse walk—back to their lands."

A young maiden showed up at the fire with a beautiful bouquet of flowers and handed it to Three Bears.

"Thank you, little one. These flowers will brighten my day."

The bouquet consisted of Firewheels, or Blanket Flowers as some called them. They were daisy-like wild flowers and vividly colored red, orange and yellow. The center is red-violet, fading to orange and then to yellow at the petal tips.

"I will hold the *Kinaalda*—Beauty Way Ceremony—for you. It may be a bit too soon in your life, but you are going to be blessed."

He received a broad smile as she skipped away.

It was becoming clear that only the young still believed in him. His *shamanistic* teachings had taken a serious set-back to the powers expected of him. They had diminished considerably by his own lack of interest.

The digs had become the center of information for him, as well.

*　　*　　*

Subsequent magnetometer surveys revealed a more complex picture than that of a simple pueblo, as first suggested. The enclosed area was perhaps ten and a half acres in size; a city-state of sorts.

Enterprising Cliff wasn't about to lose out on all the extra income provided by all the rubber-neckers as interest grew. He had Ernie running a Ford mini-bus to the site twice daily with hawk-faced newspaper people, tag-long curiosity seekers and archaeo-tourists.

They were becoming a nuisance to the workers and asking inane questions of Doc and Helene, neither of whom provided informative detailed answers.

Eva Maurer was now seen to be scrambling among the several trenches. In addition to her ever present notebook, she now was the proud owner of a small recorder, strapped to her hip in a holster.

She had been signed on as a stringer for some newspaper in Albuquerque and basking in her glory. She sported a press card and visitor's pass. They dangled from a thong around her turkey-like neck.

Eva's notes and comments were her dreams. A place to let her imagination soar. A magic world of her own.

*　　*　　*

A strange, unusual ground fog enveloped the canyon. It appeared as a low-lying cloud and gradually crept down the canyon floor.

Timco, Jack, Ruby, Han Po and Red Hawk Cooper were riding casually along the road toward the digs when Doc passed in a whirlwind of dust, driving the jeep in the opposite direction. He had completed his opus of discoveries and progress on the digs. The opus was over a hundred single-spaced, detailed pages which were interspersed with many gnomic phrases. His way of making the reading easier.

"How did you end up as a policeman, Cooper?" Ruby asked.

It wasn't the first time someone asked him that exact same question, which always sounded pejorative to him.

The best response he could muster was: "I went into the law business because I wanted to get hitched."

"What?"

"That's it. I was taking a course in law and fell for a fellow student. She was something else. I quit school and we got married. The only job I could find was with the Nation police force. We split up a few years later, but I stayed on the force. Just like that. You ever been married, Ruby?"

"Nope. Came close once but I wasn't sure it was worth the trouble."

She was all gussied up, anticipating meeting with the media and maybe having some pictures taken.

Smiling broadly, Han Po said, "*Bie chu x` in cái.* It seems like you're making a move for one Doc, with that get-up on."

"You really think so, my Chinese friend? I've been known to dress up a time or two before. Anyhow, mind your own damned business!"

Midnight was loping alongside the group when he suddenly veered off and headed for a slight depression near the riverbank.

"Something's over there," Cooper said, as he reined in. "See those ravens circling above?"

He rode over to Midnight and came upon two hawks feasting on a cadaver. A bald turkey buzzard, with a grotesque head and hooked beak, stood by, waiting it's turn on the feast. The repulsive bird, clumsy on the ground, was hissing at the intruders.

The buzzard finally taloned one of the hawks and it uttered a terrified squeal. Both hawks took off. The buzzard plunged it's beak into the stomach and extracted a long piece of succulent gut that glistened white against the scorched earth.

"What's over there?" Timco hallooed.

"See for yourself. It looks like we've located the missing Renaldo."

It was him, alright. His cyanosed lips were stretched back in agony—as though he were witnessing his own death.

His decomposing body lay in a small puddle near the riverbank. A lone frog was perched on the front of his skull, sunbathing; waiting for an anthropod or two to come within striking distance of his tongue. The male species was emitting a *ribbit* calling to attract a mate.

Unbeknownst to him, this particular puddle was vacant and he was calling in vain.

Should he stay too long in his relaxed position, eventually one of the ravens will make a *hors d' oeuvre* of him prior to resuming gorging on the carrion.

"Pretty hard to determine for certain if this is Renaldo," Cooper stated.

"Not really," Timco answered. "Notice the battery acid spots on the jeans? Not many folks around here mess with batteries."

"You're probably right."

"How long you figure he's been out here, Cooper?"

"Well, the flies feast on fresh blood and this corpse is crawling with maggots. Guessing the size of these maggots to be about fifteen millimeters, I'd say he's been out here about six days. "

"How come you know so much about this cop stuff?"

"Took the twenty-six week F.B.I. course at Quantico."

"That explains it. There's not much else we can do here. What say we ride?" Jack suggested.

"I'm not in a big hurry. Prefer using an hour glass for the time. I'll write this up before calling it in. They'll send a team down for his body. See y'all at the site later on."

"Shouldn't we move him?" Han Po asked.

"Don't matter much now. Dead's dead. Life never ends on a high note; death is the final salute," Cooper answered, a slight grin on his lips.

Chapter Forty-Four

They were hunkered down around a large, pleasing campfire. The dark blue of the far-off hills had been shaded by the deep black of night.

"Kinda strange how that feller Renaldo got murdered, ain't it?" Mike asked no one in particular. His one good eye flashed.

Timco grinned. "It's advisable for a person to die at the peak of one's obituary. It is written. And also, death is *always* replaced with a birth. Dinah's baby is a prime example, don't you think?"

"Who wrote that?"

"It was most likely me in a moment of prophesying, as I'm wont to do, at times."

"Right. Of course, I don't think Cliff understands one word of what you're saying," Doc managed, straight –faced.

Cliff bristled. "Kish meyn tokhes, Goyim!"

Midnight's snout rested on crossed paws as he watched the group through sleepy eyes. Then he was sitting up, his head tilted to one side, and raised his ears, alert.

There were sounds of a catamount screaming. He whimpered and laid back down, then went to sleep; dreaming of cats and squirrels he could be chasing.

Then a slight hesitation in conversation. Doc scribbled notes on a yellow quad pad. He initialed each page so there would be no question of apocrypha.

Timco stretched out his arms, yawned widely, and moved closer to the fire.

"Smell it?"

"What?"

"Rain's comin'," he grumbled.

Doc gave a hint of exegesis to the remark. Timco was unbearable at times. He was of a different world, it seemed.

A funereal wind, with sad rain and low clouds approached.

"It's raining pussies and puppies," Doc stated.

"You mean cats and dogs," Timco groused. He sat there for a moment, lips pulled back from his teeth, as if he were about to snarl.

"Precisely," was Doc's inane response.

Everyone made a dash for cover.

In the Quonset hut Doc and Timco sat together at the small table near the work bench, a bottle of brandy between them, waiting for a hand to grasp it.

Outside the rain was filling a small gully with a tiny, fishless creek.

Jack joined them. "Hey, tipi dweller, do me a favor and pull on my finger."

Timco reached for the appendage extending out from Jack's hand and pulled.

Jack cut loose with a magnificent fart, which sounded like a long note on a trombone.

"That's good," he announced proudly. "It relieves the pressure."

"You're rotten, you know," Timco scolded.

"I know."

Jack had flatulent plumbing.

CHAPTER FORTY-FIVE

Sunrise was a burst of color. The deep blue of night slowly gave way to a pink smudge as daybreak made an appearance.

Andoni burst into the Quonset on his short legs, gasping for breath.

"Doc! There's some mean-looking riders in camp and they're looking for trouble, I betcha."

"How many?"

"There's five or four."

"Go tell Timco and Jack. Tell 'em to come armed."

Chollo and his bandito compadres were scattering the workers with their horses, causing pandemonium and scaring hell out of the children.

Timco arrived on the scene, followed closely by Midnight.

"Get down off your horses or I'll be obliged to cut loose with this shotgun," he ordered.

Chollo's randy pard, Comacho, braving the threat, dropped out of his saddle and stood with a sneer on his lips.

Midnight, usually docile, charged him and took a sizeable chunk out of his rump.

Screaming madly, Comacho reached for his pistol, but Jack was on him in a flash. Comacho began cursing the dog while being controlled in a bear hug.

"You touch one hair on the dog and I'll be obliged to sever your manhood and feed it to the crows," Timco warned.

Chollo began to open his mouth to say something.

"And you, *Chico,* don't get your balls in an uproar. Just make tracks outta here," Timco said. "We've got better things to do than corral you bunch of no-good bastards."

*   *   *

There was a hubbub, a babel, in the Indian encampment.

Yellow Fox decided to investigate. When he arrived he encountered an emaciated specimen of a Mexican lobo that had been terrorizing the people. It ranged throughout the camp snarling and charging at any person who neared it.

He surveyed the situation. Midnight, at his side, growled menacingly and had his hackles up.

"Stay, boy. I'll handle this myself."

He neared the lobo, fists clenched in front. When the animal made a move to attack, he punched it severely on the snout. It loped away yipping like a newborn pup.

A woman came up to him, all smiles, and planted a wet kiss on his cheek.

"You're so brave, Yellow Fox. You saved my child from disaster."

"It was nothing, young mother. The animal was hungry and I doubt it would have harmed anyone. It was far from home and most likely lost. All is quiet now."

*   *   *

Doctor Piquette, accompanied by an anthropologist, Professor A. G. Bell, arrived later that morning. His gold tooth caught the sun's rays like a searchlight.

She had the lab results from the findings of a few days ago. Most were classified as chordates. Two species of the fossils included vertebrates which were regarded as fish.

There was one small piece of bone that had interested the Professor and he wanted to investigate the area more fully. After his introduction, Doc asked, "Your initials. Do they stand for Alexander Graham?"

"Not likely. He's long gone. You must have me confused with Don Ameche. My name is Arthur George."

"Of course, how dense of me."

He turned to Dr. Piquette. "I see you've brought along your own driver. What's his name?"

"Oh, that's Soybean Brown, my lab assistant."

"Good show. We can always use another sturdy body."

CHAPTER FORTY-SIX

There was a chilly snap to the air. Fall was dancing on the fringes of winter. Frenchy cut loose with a loud yell.

"What's with you?" Ole asked.

"A scorpion nailed me."

"Where'd it get ya?"

"Well, if I was walking north, you might say it got me on the south side."

Ole smiled. "Don't sweat it, friend. Your body mass will prevent any real damage. Besides, of the fourteen hundred species of scorpions only thirty are harmful to humans. You've been snagged by one not of the thirty."

"Thanks a bunch, Mr. Oleson. It's still gonna be hell sitting down."

The north facing door was now clear of debris. Doc's shovel struck something solid.

"You there! Ralph! Give me a hand and let's see what we've got here."

In a few minutes a large cylindrical object was uncovered.

"I'll be got to hell!" Doc exclaimed. "What we have here is a genuine Toltec calendar."

He went on to explain that the Toltec's calendar ran in a cycle of fifty-two years of 260 days each. Their empire collapsed in the 13th century when the Aztecs defeated them.

Their prophecies said we—the whites—are at the bottom of the ninth hell. They warned that light-skinned ones with flowing beards would return to conquer them and claim the land as their own. I suppose they meant the Spanish who came in the 1400's on the exact day shown on this calendar of stone.

"When Dr. Piquette gets back tomorrow she'll be very interested in this find, I'm sure."

In the meantime, Ruth Golden Eagle was cleaning out an area rich in Clovis points. The Clovis and other Paleoindian point forms dated from a period around 13,500 years ago.

Clovis points were created by a process called *flint knapping* whereby percussion by a hammer stone or antler billet removed flakes from the flint, chert or other stone material. A groove was made along the point permitting it to be attached to shafts or spears.

The spear would be thrown by hand or with an *atatl,* a device whereby the spear is set in a hollowed out shaft, with a cup at one end, in which the butt of the spear rests. Use of this simple tool by the hunter provided greater velocity.

Billy Stillwell was given the task of building an additional work bench in the Quonset. With the large collection of artifacts being uncovered, there just wasn't enough space on the original bench.

Along with Justin, there were now two other overseers from the museum categorizing each find as it reached the surface. It wasn't so much there was fear of pilferage, the cataloguing was necessary for historical verification.

* * *

With help from Ole and Frenchy, progress on the mound was showing results. Vestigal traces of a structure were appearing. The front of an anagama-style kiln was now visible. Yellow Fox presented a sample of charcoal to Doc.

"It's apparent this kiln was used for firing pots and other ceramic items," he observed. "The ancient peoples used cow, sheep or horse dung, mixed with sawdust and wood chips to provide the heat necessary for firing material, such as clay."

"Now that this site has been verified, where do you want us now?" Yellow Fox asked.

"Let me think on it for a bit. Take your group over to the kitchen and have some coffee or something."

Andoni and Eddur were at it again. There was a slab of pie on the table, left over from last night's meal.

Edur, in a state of commiseration for his slow-witted brother, said, "You cut and I'll choose first."

"What if you get the biggest piece, like you always do?"
"Think about it, numb nuts. If you cut it evenly we both get a good hunk."

"Yeh. Guess you're right."

On the other side of the room, two of the student helpers were involved in a heated argument.

"Well, smart ass, my uncle is an airline pilot but *I* can't fly. My arms get too tired," he smirked.

"Big deal! My uncle is a veterinarian, but *I* can't bark or scratch my ass with my leg."

Timco heard enough. "Out! The whole damned bunch of you! Get over to the ditch where Ruth Golden Eagle is digging and work up a sweat!"

CHAPTER FORTY-SEVEN

Hotar and Yellow Fox were relaxing together; backs against a pile of dirt.

Hotar was a robust personage. He crossed his legs at the ankles. He was so afraid of being wrong that he was usually wrong.

"Any of your old pals still around, Yellow Fox?"

"Not hardly. The ones that didn't drink themselves to death headed out for concrete country. The ones here now feel strange to me. They all get along with my ex-wife though. She has her way of dealing with people."

Hotar's craggy face took on a grimace. "I've got the finest kind of a toothache and raging hemorrhoids. Might have to make a speed run to see a dentist."

He ran his fingers through his thick, stiff hair in an effort to comb it.

Doc sidled up. "I've noticed the dilatoriness of our native inhabitants has increased recently, Timco. Can you do something about it? It's really irritating me."

"I'll mention it to Dragonfly. That's how it's done. How's it going in the hut?"

"We're coming along nicely. Dr. Piquette is a genius when it comes to classifying. She believes some of the items stem from the Phoenicians."

"You're shittin' me!"

"Not at all. Some historians propose that the Phoenicians traveled by ship from Lebanon to the sea that covered this whole area thousands of years ago. We're going to send samples to New Mexico University for radiocarbon testing."

"I'll be go to hell!"

*   *   *

Three Bears and the young one came near.

"We will be on our way, friend Yellow Fox. Too long in one place and I become vegetated."

"I hate to see you go. You've been a welcome change around here. Mebbee our paths will cross again, hunh?"

"Mebbee so." He touched the brim of his hat in salute.

Standing in his shadow, Three Fingers followed suit—imitating the old man.

Three Bears entered life reluctantly and withdrew from it whenever necessary or possible. He was a lone man and didn't need an audience.

His side-kick, Three Fingers, was becoming anxious to move on also. The sun beat down on his back. He removed his shirt. He was thin. His shoulder blades formed a triangle, similar to the radioactive signs on the rear of some trucks.

And then, they were off. They didn't take the road to town. Their direction was northeast, across the nothing land. There were tufts of grass combed by the wind. Their spavined horse, loaded with the tent and a few personal items, struggled along, a short pace behind the travelers.

*   *   *

There was activity at the diggings. Successive layers of debris from centuries of human habitat were encountered.

Yellow Fox's group uncovered a large area of bones, some distance from the center of the imagined town.

"I think we've dug up some horse—and possibly some camel bones. There's also a spear tip carved from obsidian and a glob of something that looks like petrified shit," he mentioned to Doc.

"Is that so?"

"That's my opinion. I've heard they had camels around here a long time ago."

"Everyone has a right to their opinion—just so it agrees with mine," Doc said sarcastically. "Before you get too excited, I'll have Dr. Piquette and the professor take a look."

"Whatever you say, Doc. You're the boss."

"You've got that right, and don't forget it. Why don't you take your crew over to the barracks and relax for awhile. Then we can verify these finds without interference."

"Yeh. You wouldn't want us peons around to contaminate this stuff. Anyway, I've got to mix up some batter for biscuits. Wouldn't want you *professionals* going hungry."

While they were talking, Ruth Golden Eagle shouted from deep within the excavation.

"Mr. Doc! Come quick! We found a skeleton!"

The two doctors and the professor rushed over to see what had caused such excitement. First to scramble down into the hole was professor Bell. He shooed all the workers away and began to uncover the bones.

"Eureka!" he shouted. "What we have here is a coclophysis in almost perfect form."

"Sure it is," Doc said. "You took the word right out of my mouth."

"Bull shit!" Timco mouthed with a wide grin from the rim of the excavation. These professionals are something else, [he thought].

The coelophysis, it seems, was a comparatively small carnivore of the Triassic Period, some 222-215 million years ago.

It's maximum length was about ten feet and it weighed a meager one hundred pounds of so.

In recent years it has been designated as the New Mexico State Fossil. Hundreds of skeletons were located in one remote area called, Ghost Ranch, where they probably concentrated in a group seeking food and water.

*   *   *

Up until the time of the findings, there had been a laissez-faire attitude by the State, allowing Doc considerable latitude in running the project. Now, in addition to Justin, there were two full-time rent-a-cops patrolling the site. There were also restraining ropes surrounding many of the trenches to keep inquisitive people at bay.

Han Po stood above the most recent trench, arms folded across his meager chest, head slightly tilted to one side.

Timco walked up to him. "How in hell did you get this close to the digs, Han Po?"

"One of those gun-toting guards began to stop me, but I gave him the Chinese one-fingered salute and told him I was an inspector."

"Okay, I guess. Just be careful. It's a long way down to the bottom and the sides aren't all that stable."

"Yes. It seems so. *M`o ming gi mia `o*. The wonder and mystery of it all," he beamed.

"You can say that again."

"The wonder and—."

"Forget I brought it up, you oriental joker."

"That is good. It reminds me of a Lao-tzu saying: "He who knows, does not speak—he who speaks, does not know.""

Hotar, the sidewinder, the stub of a cigar dangling from his mouth, hollered up that he'd have to stop. "Send down some more shovel people. I ran into another wall that looks like it has a door in it."

Billy Stillwell, eager to get into the mix, took four others and went down the side of the trench as though he were rappelling. They soon had a large space cleared. There was a door. The door was sealed tightly and they decided to wait instructions.

Doc hallooed down to the group to stand by until they could determine a way to enter without disturbing anything.

Timco examined the door and said they should first drill a small hole in it with a chisel to ensure there weren't any poisonous gases within. He knew of some Egyptian tombs where the archaeologists were overcome. A few died. Best to use caution.

Jack took on the chore of drilling, and soon had a two-inch hole through. Using a small flashlight Doc peered into the chamber behind the door and shouted, "The air's stale, but it seems to be free of any gas. This is fantastic!"

He took several deep breaths before continuing.

"The room seems to have remained as it was since the day it was sealed. No apparent damage. I can see part of a frescoed wall and several items scattered around the floor. Let's get this door out of the way so we can investigate further."

Bully Stillwell made short work of the task.

Professor Bell stood at the entrance and exclaimed, "This is the greatest find since Schliemann ravaged the gold of Troy!"

Doc Cambrensis, Dr. Piquette and professor Bell stood in awe just inside the room. The fresco on the opposite wall was in almost perfect condition. It depicted a dozen men and women, all quite tall, with flaxen hair. Several children were also shown. All the clothing had a trim of azure blue. Lapis lazuli appeared to have been used in the dye.

One of the women was drawn with her hand on a child's breast. Dr. Piquette explained that in some ancient cultures the milking of an infants breast was supposed to contribute to a shapely breast in adulthood. Another woman held a jar in her upraised hand, apparently filled with an aromatic cream to be applied to her breasts; her nipples were painted with a red rouge.

Lactating women were revered for their life-giving nutrients, Piquette mentioned. She was an expert at reconstructing ancient civilizations; some as far back as 6,000 years.

"There's an old adage that states women have breasts to make suckers out of men," Doc said with a sly grin.

As they proceeded cautiously deeper into the room, hundreds of containers of various sizes were found scattered about. One large terracotta jar, with a brownish-orange color, turned out to hold terebinth resin, probably of Canaanite origin. Another container held traces of cosmetic henna, remarkably well preserved.

"That's very strange," Piquette observed.

"Why so?" Bell asked.

"That particular cosmetic is native to regions of Africa, southern Asia and northern Australia. It doesn't quite fit with these frescos. These people appear to be Semitic.

Perfumed unguents were found in another container. Once the clay stopper was removed, the residual odor was still apparent.

A clay jar containing the wax of a honey comb was located on a small shelf. An offering to some god or goddess? Cuneiform symbols etched thereon were not of this hemisphere. Also, honey bees were not native to the Americas, as thought previously. They were brought in from Asia and Europe. A change in thinking would be necessary after these findings.

"It appears this site has been used by several civilizations over the centuries," Bell said. "It's truly an amazing find!"

A halt was called to any further diggings as several specimens were taken to the Quonset for further examination.

CHAPTER FORTY-EIGHT

It was a fall-winter day in which some oaks still managed to cling to their leaves, while others were completely bare.

One of the workers was bitten on the ankle by a rattler that didn't realize it was time to hibernate. A fellow worker pinned it's head to the ground with a shovel and then cut off a portion of meat, applying it to the wound. This would draw out the venom.

Jack and Timco were relaxing over mugs of coffee and pieces of pie.

"You know, Jack, we don't inherit the land from our ancestor—we borrow it from our children. That's an old Native American proverb."

"Sure it is. In your case though, you *bought* it from your children."

"How's that?"

"You're only half Indian."

"What the hell do you know about picking blueberries in Nova Scotia?"

"Not a damned thing. What's that gotta do with anything?"

"Ah, piss off! Pass me another slab of that pie. Anyhow, you know that Renaldo guy wasn't killed at the garage?"

"How so?"

"No grease on his hands."

"Pretty clever, Sherlock."

"I manage. It's the way of the Dené to observe things like that."

"Who woulda thunk it? You're so damned clever, you should run for Governor."

"No way, José! They'd figure out real fast that I wouldn't listen to their crap and most likely go on a scalping spree."

"Yeh. Right. You know, Timco, the longer I stay out west the more I enjoy the people. Very few phonies. Back east most people regard westerners as complete rubes—still fighting savages and living in soddies. Shows how much those snot-noses know, doesn't it?"

"You said it. Those people to the east of the Mississippi have always needed an attitude adjustment."

"You know what bugs me the most, Jack? Since Three Bears left, it's my not knowing the proper ceremonial procedures. I was getting sorta used to joining in again. I remember one of them that cracked me up.

"In the old days when the mother-in-law or grandmother farted, the young bride had to collect the gas and save it. That ritual is long gone now."

"What a pity."

CHAPTER FORTY-NINE

A short way southwest of the central scheme, in a small four by six foot trash-filled room, and adjacent to a midden, more than 200 miniature pots and other replicas were located.

Consultants suggested these small vessels might have been toys for children, or placed in kilns to ensure good firing, or used in ceremonies or for holding pigments, or to contain corn pollen.

They didn't know squat!

Out place in this room was a jar that held a sample of amaranth—a food grain grown along with corn and beans—and two small cenotaphs.

Dragonfly made one of her infrequent visits to the site and mentioned to Doc that the name for this area is *kaach-ta-kaact,* meaning wide area of buildings.

"They didn't abandon this place. It's still occupied. The spirits are everywhere."

She paused. A frown on her brow.

"You must believe everything has a spirit, then you'll think twice before harming anything."

"I'm not too sharp when it comes to preserving this stuff," Jack said, "But from what I hear, they'll crate most of it up and haul it to the museum in Albuquerque. The good things will be cleaned up and put on display."

"That will be alright if they handle it properly. Do you know if they'll have a shaman present?"

"I really don't know, Dragonfly, but I'll check into it. I'll find out for you."

"Thank you, Jack Collins."

*   *   *

Although Doc still had carte blanche to oversee the project as he saw fit, he was feeling somewhat contrite when they started to load up the artifacts. He realized they would have to shut down soon for the winter, but he still felt bad the Indians had to be let go—back to the rez. They did a marvelous job.

Word was circulating that there would be a farewell pow-pow once everything at the site had been secured. Guards would be present continuously until operations resumed once more in the spring. Yellow Fox was to oversee making the Quonset ready and available for them.

A hawk was prowling the wind, searching for a meal.

*   *   *

Dragonfly sat by Yellow Fox near the stove. She was quiet for a long time. Then, without looking at him, she said, "Some people make us feel dark. We need canaries and headlamps like in a coal mine to find our safe way."

"You're worried about them taking all the artifacts away, aren't you? They're experts at this sort of thing, and will take very good care of your ancestor's belongings. When everything is catalogued and cleaned, it will be ready for display so that everyone can enjoy. You'll see."

"I'm sure you're right, but I still don't feel happy about it. The old ways will never be the same."

"Not to worry so much. Happiness is a myth, Dragonfly. It was invented to make us buy things. It's a crutch to cover sadness. You'll see things differently when you return home."

"The elders speak of the ancestral people who have gone through this land. This is where our oral tradition comes from and we want to keep it alive."

Yellow Fox was aware of the Archaeological Resources Protection Act which prohibits anyone from removing artifacts or disturbing archaeological sites on Federal Lands without written permission from the B.L.M., however, this particular site didn't come under those regulations. It is part of a land grant.

The specific requirements laid down by the museum and the State were definitive enough to ensure everything would be handled with the greatest care.

He placed a hand on her shoulder as she made her way back to the campground, head bowed.

Chapter Fifty

Preparations were underway to hold the ceremonial pow-wow that would announce the end of the project for the season. Yellow Fox was nominated as the master-of-ceremonies. It would be his responsibility to keep singers, dancers and those in attendance informed as to the schedule of events and to maintain the drum rotation.

The women were busy preparing a variety of food. There were some making kneel-down bread and *neeshjizhi*. Others were in the process of building delicious Indian tacos and frybread. Along with the normal corn batter, amaranth was added to the traditional batter; the flowers of which were made into dye by the Hopi—a deep red dye.

Almost all of the victuals held in the larder were dispensed as none could be returned to the commodity warehouse.

There were drums, singing and dancing.

Then there was the drum that sang a song that invited anyone who wanted, to dance. It would be the *intertribal dance*. Hotar put on a magnificent display to the accompaniment of the host drum.

The setting sun was like a funeral fire with flares of cerise and magenta—eventually fading into evening and the first silent stars of the soft night.

It was late. Yellow Fox sat alone in the Quonset, contemplating his navel. He didn't hear her come in.

She stood in the light and with an impish grin began to unbutton her shirt.

"You're somewhat of an adventurous person, aren't you? What does that suggest?"

"That I'll try almost anything."

"Correct. Give me five."

He sat there stunned.

"Turn around," she says. "Close your eyes."

He turns around, obedient as a rookie.

"Doctor Piquette—he begins—."

Then in a very quiet voice, she says, "Turn around. Open your eyes. Do you like what you see?"

"Hell yes!"

She stood there with her shirt off. Her jeans and boots were in a pile on the floor. Nothing but some flimsy white underthings making an attempt to cover the white that hadn't been browned by sunlight.

"Say yes, Timco."

He has a hard time with that simple word, but then he's following her to the cot in the rear, where she grabs him by the belt.

"I feel like nun who's been cloistered. Don't say anything, just pleasure me."

CHAPTER FIFTY-ONE

Ralph came charging over to Yellow Fox in a real tizzy.

"That squirrely savage has compromised my hard drive!"

"The hell, you say," Yellow Fox answered with a grimace.

"He was beatin' on the keys like they was bongo drums!"

"I'm thinking he's never seen anything like your laptop before, and maybe figured it would provide him with some music."

"How damned stupid! He's probably never even watched TV either!"

"Relax, Ralph. He's just an overgrown child."

At six-foot two and two hundred pounds, no less!

*   *   *

There was a barricade across the road with a formal sign warning trespassers they would be prosecuted. The archaeological site was now under the control of State guards.

The Estancia and it's environs were now in a state of flux as all the reporters, rubber-neckers and the usual professional moochers were leaving in droves. They would be back in the spring, ready to be bothersome as gnats.

There were those dying of cancer or leprosy or syphilis—depending on who told the story—but they were a close-knit mob.

*   *   *

They were holding a critique in the café.

The air outside was full of tiny flakes of snow that swirled and fluttered..

"Holy sardines! You see that? It's damned snow!" Doc said, exasperated. That'll sure put a damper on any further digging."

"What you mean, Doc, is holy mackerel, and yes indeed, it's snow," Timco mentioned casually.

"You had a female in the Quonset, Timco?" Doc asked cautiously.

"No!" *How in hell had he found out?*

"Of course, I understand. The unique pleasure of the solitary method, if I may say so, is often preferable. There's always the question of hygiene, not to mention speed," he grinned. "It's a rational choice. Still, a helping hand wouldn't be amiss. Between friends, it's often the most civilized way to relieve oneself."

"Bull shit, Doc!"

Jack had heard enough. "I'm heading out for awhile. Catch you guys later."

The only life left in the room was contained in the cobwebs. No one spoke for what seemed an eternity. More coffee was ordered. It was ten minutes to the hour on this Sunday morning.

They sipped at their mugs in anticipation of the hour to strike. The ancient clock on the back wall didn't disappoint.

The snow was now cascading, being urged along by a bitter wind. It was one of those strange desert storms; lightning, thunder, rain, sleet, snow along with a strong odor of ozone.

Don Mauer came staggering in, blowing air out between chapped lips. His hands appeared to have chilblains. He had been moving his wares from the sidewalk into the store.

"I seen the craziest thing just now. There were these zig-zag tracks in the snow leading up to the door of that abandoned shack up the street. None leaving. You don't suppose someone went in through the doggie door, do ya?"

"Mebbee a couple of us should eyeball that, huh?" Hotar asked. "Be somethin' to do."

A dog entrance, or doggie door, as they were commonly called, led into the front room. Of course, there hadn't been a dog around that place for quite some time.

The mystery was solved. It seems that Conchita, in her drunken stupor, crawled through the opening to get out of the raging blizzard. She was found curled into a fetal position, dead as a doornail. Her hands were clasped firmly together, clamped between her legs. Her flimsy clothing was frozen to her body.

"Might as well leave her be," Hotar said. "Stiff as she is, she'll keep until we can notify officer Cooper to get someone to haul her away."

"Now that's very touching," Don said, teeth chattering.

"Well, hell, man, what would you suggest?"

"You're probably right. Let's get back to the café and warm up."

They explained the situation to Doc. "Why don't you just prop her up in the middle of the street to act as a traffic cop?" he offered without too much feeling.

"What are you, Doc, some kind of screwy head-shrinker?"

"No, but you know, they make psychologists get analyzed before they certify them."

"You're a certifiable nut case, yourself, you know that Doc," Timco chimed in.

The conversation returned to the digs.

"I would guess we're smack-dab in the middle of that village," Doc said. "Once we got to digging it was all structured for us to discover those ruins."

"I'll go along with that thinking," Timco added. "It seems to spread out to the southwest."

"Yeh. And did you notice how the walls in that first room were made from identical-sized blocks of sandstone and joined with a clay-like mortar? Pretty damned good engineering if you ask me," Hotar mentioned.

"That's just the point," Doc said. "I believe we've uncovered more than one civilization, but there's no way of knowing until Dr. Piquette comes up with some radiocarbon verifications and we resume digging in the spring."

"I'll sure want to be there to find out," Timco said.

Hotar nodded.

"How about Jack? Anyone hear of his plans?" Doc questioned.

"Nope. Tight-lipped since we came to town. Figure he'll let us know soon enough," Timco replied. "I saw him checking over his truck, so maybe he's ready to head out."

*　　*　　*

They had been on the trail for three days since leaving the digs. Their noses were pointed northeast. The weather had a bite to it. Almost cold.

Walking into the sun felt good on Three Bear's tired body. Every once in a while his feet would kick up a fat grasshopper, making it trundle off. Three Fingers straggled, rather than walked, on tender feet over hunks of dead grass and past the thorns of mesquite.

"Hell, it wasn't far to the next place, was it?" Three Bears wondered. "We spent too much time around civilization and got soft," he complained to the wild country.

Chasing your shadow is almost as rewarding as a dog chasing his own tail.

*　　*　　*

"Agnes, why do most women lift a leg when they're being kissed? Seems to me they'd lose their balance."

"I really don't know. Maybe so their bodies can get closer together?"

They stood in the center of the room, waiting for something. Then she stepped back and shed her clothes. It was like she was peeling a peach of it's skin. They came off easily.

He stood next to her, cocked his head, and listened.

"It sounds bad outside."

The blizzard was howling a mournful tune, snow swirling, attacking the door. He caught the scent of her and it stirred up a sort of jealousy. Other times with other women. He felt like he was about to betray her. He was intoxicated with her; it was the rarest of all sensations.

He took her by the elbow and led her to the bedroom.

When they had made hungry love, she rolled on her side and asked, "I hear you might be baling out, Jack. Any truth to it?"

Here we go again [he thought].

"Haven't made up my mind yet. You probably have a clue that I've got itchy feet."

He rolled off his side of the bed, and reached for a smoke.

"It's not that I don't have strong feelings for you, but that's just the way I am."

"Okay then, I won't try to chain you down. Get your butt back into bed so I can rape you. '

CHAPTER FIFTY-TWO

The late Indian summer overlapped into November. The autumn sunlight in it's feeble, pellucid attitude, provided little warmth.

"You hear that?" Hotar asked.

"Sure, it's the new church bell," Don mentioned casually.

"Well, I'm a secular person, but that bell is purely righteous," Timco said.

His words were as in iambic pentameter form. To ward off the cold, he was clad in a heavy cloth anorak, with drawstrings tipped with deer antler, in the style of his far northern relations.

"It surely does make the church seem more legal when that bell sounds," Hotar beamed.

Jack sat up straighter in his chair. His accomplishments didn't go unnoticed. His chest puffed out in pride. Still his secret if Cliff didn't blab.

Doc swiveled around to face the Bengolarrea twins at the adjacent table. He studied Edur for a second or two.

"That growth on your brother's neck seems to be benign, Andoni."

Andoni wasn't paying attention. His face was inches away from a plate of liver and onions.

"What do you mean he's benign, Doc? Everyone knows you'll be nine after you be eight."

The growth had a personality of it's own. It had whiskers like a Grand Banks fisherman.

"Forget I mentioned it," Doc sad exasperated. "What plans do you two have now?"

"We'll probably hunt up a sheep ranch to tide us over the winter. They're always looking for herders."

"Sounds reasonable, considering your ethnic backgrounds. You'll both have positions at the digs in the spring, if you want."

"That'll be just fine, Doc. Thanks."

CHAPTER FIFTY-THREE

He awoke with a start. Heart pounding against his ribs. He blessed himself backwards—an act of compunction. A habit he picked up from his grandfather who performed it thusly whenever he was excited or worried. After which he postulated ferociously to the heavens and would proclaim that poverty makes whores of us all.

His grandfather would come down to Long Island from New Rochelle two or three times a year, seeking refuge, he would announce, from wanton women chasing after his fortune; of which there was a definite lack.

He would arrive each time in the same threadbare clothing; a secret smile on his lips, a twinkle in his eyes and a hint of blarney for all.

Last night's dream had been a real doozie. He tried to yell but no sound came out. He massaged his larynx to try to get some action out of the damned thing.

It refused to comply.

His eyes were closed tightly with an image of him as a youngster which he recalled so vividly he could have been experiencing it in that moment. He prevented himself from falling back to sleep so his memories didn't become dreams and run from his control.

He remembered his mother patting his butt with an oversized powder puff filled with talcum.

And, the first step he ever took.

Of getting everyone excited thinking he was lost. He had only been investigating the small copse at the rear of the property. He always had a good sense of direction.

He was experiencing the corrupting force of dreams. The ultimate lie. He found that in his dreams he was posthumously reliving a parodic version of awakened desires; that life consisted above all, a waiting to be possessed; bringing every happiness and every grief.

For the first time his dream had a meaning. Perhaps it was only an echo, but he was determined, in his mind, to think only good thoughts.

*   *   *

A monstrous six-foot tumbleweed came merrily down main street waiting to join it's neighbors in happy declaration. It eventually lodged itself onto the door frame of the café.

Activity around town had dwindled to slow walks and mute whisperings.

"Jack, it seems you're making plans to head out," Doc mentioned, a frown creasing his brow.

"Yup. I can't see hanging around here all winter with nothing to do. I thought I might head out tomorrow."

"I figured you might like it around here enough to stick with it."

"Hey, I'm not going anywhere where they do things with the dead, like at the digs. When it comes to doing things, I prefer people to be alive—and female. You people can dig all you want around that ancient graveyard, but not this guy!"

Timco smiled. "Anyhow, Jack, just remember, the closest point between two friends—is a smile. Try it. As for me, I've got some unfinished business with Dr. Piquette."

"Aren't you a bit old for her?"

"No sweat! Her specialty being the study of fossils, I figure I fit right in, yeh?"

*　　*　　*

He was filling his thermos in the café. Many of the patrons and his close acquaintances were standing around, looks of concern on their faces. Juanita had a single tear making a snail-like trail down a cheek.

The weather wasn't conducive to traveling.

"You sure you want to head out in this crappy weather, Jack?" Doc asked.

"It's now or never. The longer I wait, the harder it's going to be to leave you folks."

Large Ruby embraced him, almost staving in his ribs.

"You're staying, Timco?"

"Yup. Me and Midnight decided."

Doc reached into a jacket pocket and extracted a manila envelope.

"This came in yesterday from Dr. Piquette. She mentions that radiocarbon dating proved her initial reactions to the site being a combination of several cultures.

"She writes that those skeletons weren't slain as previously thought, but most likely died from a strange vector, most likely a haematophagous type.

"What's that mean in common talk, Doc?" Timco asked.

"The way it was explained to me is, it was just like the wind. You can feel it, but you can't see it."

"Now, that's some weird shit," Hotar exclaimed.

"Sure is."

"That all you got to say about the whole thing?" Don asked.

"Well, Mr. Maurer, I've found if you try too hard to articulate, you have a tendency to trip over your own tongue. I prefer explaining things in a simple way to the uninitiated. Besides, Don, I notice your store has taken on a pastiche following the recent influx of customers."

"Sure. Glad you noticed. Figured with all the extra folks running around with coins in their jeans, I might as well get sorta up to date."

The door burst open, allowing a drift of snow and a chilling wind to enter. A young Indian boy came to their table. His eyebrows and hair were caked with snow and his cheeks were glowing red.

"Dragonfly told me to bring this to you, come hell or high water, Yellow Fox. She said it was made with love from all the elders."

He was presented with a beautiful dream catcher.

"You must tell the elders thank you very much. Anyway, how in hell did you get here in this weather?"

"I rode in on my horse. He didn't like it. It was a bad trip."

"I'll bet it was. Take the animal down to the stables before it freezes to death. Then come back here for a hot meal and wait for the storm to pass."

Yellow Fox would continue his quest. After all, who else would protect the souls of those in the digs with Dragonfly gone?

They stood just outside the café door. Timco's neck muscles straining to hold his head erect. His eyes, slightly damp, were crusting over from the cold.

There were three horses, rigged vaquero-style, hitched to the rail, swishing their tails to rid them of snow.

Jack swiveled and started down the street toward the barn and his truck.

"Ah-dee-oze, Timco," he managed through pursed lips.

"You never did learn the language, Anglo." Timco chuckled. "So long, Jack. Don't get too old before I see you again."

At that precise moment he had to sneeze, and of course, you can't sneeze with your eyes open, so he missed his last chance to see Jack as he faded into the gloomy distance.

Jack's reply was lost in the howling wind. Frigid snow crystals blasted his face like birdshot.

CHAPTER FIFTY-FOUR

He was climbing slowly on a sloping three-percent grade out of the low mesa countryside into the foothills.

A slate-gray sky hovered over the early winter-dead foliage.

He gripped the steering wheel firmly, knuckles turning white. Going was a bit tricky on the snow-packed road. There was no turning back.

He was determined to continue before he had second thoughts.

The urge to relieve himself was stronger that the will to continue. He pulled into a slow-vehicle passing zone. There was a small, not yet frozen creek close by, and he stood there emptying his bladder, shivering.

As he stepped back to zip up, he lost his balance on a slippery rock and was suddenly waist deep in the frigid water. The instant shock shrunk up his privates like a turtle pulling it's head back into the shell.

There was a sudden jolt of a mistake in judgment as he climbed the bank to relative safety. On this deserted stretch of highway, in this rotten weather, it would have been prudent to just piss near the truck, being careful not to soak his shoes.

Rummaging through his duffle bag, he located dry clothes and changed rapidly before he became a human icicle, unable to move, waiting for the spring thaw.

*   *   *

Yellow Fox sat by himself in the café. He was contemplating the expending of his energy for another season on the digs.

Three Bears had presented him with a catlinite pipe bowl with a long stem. The bowl was made of an opaque terra-cotta colored stone; more commonly known as pipestone. With little ceremony he filled the bowl and smoked it.

Yellow Fox was tired of floundering around like a flounder—although he wasn't exactly certain which one of the over one hundred species of flounder applied to his dilemma.

Hopefully, his decision to remain at the digs would be beneficial and somewhat symbolic in nature. His Navajo genes were overriding the Norwegian chromosomes.

He was reflecting on tid-bits of information received from the old ones— Dragonfly and Three Bears. Also, the twins had explained, that in the Basque way, high up in the Pyranees mountains, their ancestors helped to carry forward tradition of what is good, true and beautiful.

Han Po entered the café and homesteaded a chair at Timco's table. They nodded greetings and remained mute.

The front door was thrown open with a crash. Chollo and two of his sidekicks stomped in, shaking snow off their boots. Yellow Fox scrunched up his brow at this intrusion.

"Shag ass," he said without looking up, "before I skin the lot of you like snakes."

Chollo glanced at his compadres with a look of caution.

"Don't mess with the breed. He's got the cajones to do as he says."

Yellow Fox made a move to get up. "Damned straight! And if you're not outta here before I blink once more, the shit's going to hit the fan."

His jaw muscles clamped down, his eyes glared.

Han Po asked, "You doin' alright, Timco?"

Timco lifted his coffee mug only slightly before answering.

"I've had better feelings going eye to eye with a rattler."

"Fornicate the bastards, and the horses they rode in on. They're nothing but trouble and not worth the effort, friend," Han Po exclaimed.

"You're right, as usual, Han Po. Those bums just seem to get my hackles up."

The banditos left him with the memory of a large gash on his left arm—blood gushing out—received from a hunk of shrapnel on Saipan. The wound eventually healed, although leaving a nasty-looking scar.

Considering recent events—or nonevents—his was a reasonably stable life.

Few real worries. Life's a bitch, and then we die.

He just might hibernate for the winter in the cantina, listening to words of wisdom emoted by his oriental companion.